THE WATCHER
IN THE WOODS

The Watcher
in the Woods

by

Charlotte Bond

BLACK SHUCK
SHADOWS

Black Shuck Books
www.BlackShuckBooks.co.uk

A version of *The Wild Hunt* first appeared in *The Spinetinglers Anthology* (Spinetinglers Elite Publishing, 2008)

Cover design & internal layout © WHITEspace 2020
www.white-space.uk

First published in the UK by Black Shuck Books, 2020

978-1-913038-45-8

9
Hessian Sky

43
A Wolf in the House

77
The Wild Hunt

115
Teeth in the Shadows

149
The Watcher in the Woods

193
Author's Note

To the two Steves in my life:

Steve Upham,
for taking a chance on me as I was then

Steve Shaw,
for taking a chance on me as I am now

Hessian Sky

Petra had no idea where she was. It should have been simple: leave the airport at Keflavik, head south on Route 41 then onto Route 427 for about an hour to reach Strandakirkja.

'Just two goddamn roads,' she muttered under her breath. 'How could I mess that up so badly?'

Yet somehow, this simplest of trips had gone horribly wrong. With a fog suddenly blowing in from the ocean, she could barely see the road in front of her, never mind the roadside signs that might give her a hint as to her location.

A couple of times, she had considered stopping next to a sign and matching the name on it to the map in the glovebox. But the headlights on her rented car kept flickering, and she had a horrible suspicion that if she stopped the car it might not start again.

'I'll keep going. I'll find somewhere, eventually.' Her voice gathered strength as she worked through her pep talk. 'I mean, how hard can it be? My bloody job title is Creative Solutions Architect. *I'm* the one they call when everyone else has messed up. I am *not* the sort of person who gets defeated by a bit of fog.' Her voice was loud yet controlled by the time she finished, and she felt a little more grounded.

People had told her about the emptiness of Iceland out beyond the cities and settlements; she'd thought it would be a bit like Dartmoor. She hadn't expected this vast, desolate landscape.

Before the fog had settled in, she'd seen the volcanic plains stretching away to her left and the wide sea to her right. A wave of vulnerability had washed over her, and her hands had trembled slightly as they clutched the steering wheel.

Now, a headache was building behind her eyes, gradually sapping her energy. The headlights flickered again and she felt her stomach lurch.

Please, God, don't let this damn car die on me.

Suddenly the car gave a judder that shook her

bones, and then there was no sound at all as it glided to a stop. Petra stared at a dashboard twinkling with warning lights. Panic set in as she tried and failed to restart the car. She pressed every button she could see, turning on the hazard lights and the windscreen wipers before she had the presence of mind to put the handbrake on. After that, she rested her forehead on the steering wheel.

Shit. Shit. Shit.

Petra waited until the pounding in her head had eased enough to let her think straight, then she gazed out of the windscreen at a blanket of white mist.

I thought they said fog was rare in Iceland. She forced that half-formed memory away. Creative Solution Architects dealt with what was, not what should be.

Okay. First thing. Let's get the car going. Several twists of the key and numerous swear words had no effect.

Right. Next thing then. Location. She glanced at the sat nav, which told her she was apparently in the middle of a field. She rummaged in the bag next to her and drew out her phone. It concurred that she was in the middle of a field.

'Shit.'

She pulled the door handle and an alarm screamed at her for opening the door with the headlights still switched on.

'Piss off,' she muttered, thumping the lights off with more force than was necessary.

That was a mistake. The fog had been eerie when illuminated, but without the headlights on, it seemed to press closer. Petra shuddered, huddling next to the open door. With her line of sight restricted to less than a foot ahead of her, all her other senses started to overcompensate. She could taste the mist on her lips, salty and bitter. She could smell the sharp scent of the nearby ocean. And she could hear... music?

She listened harder, thinking it might just be the thud of her heartbeat, but there was the definite thump of a baseline. A bark of relieved laughter burst from her mouth, sounding uncomfortably loud in the suffocating mist.

For a long minute, she considered her options, but there was really only one viable choice. Walking around the car, she saw that she'd drifted dangerously close to the edge and was almost on the verge. Ironically, that was good, as it meant the car was mostly out of the road. She turned off the engine but left the hazard lights on.

At least I won't be responsible for causing someone's death.

Fetching her single suitcase from the boot, she scribbled a short message on a piece of paper: "Car broke down, trying to find help. Hope you don't read this because you crashed into the back of me." As she stuck it under the windscreen wiper, she wondered if she should try to write a note in Icelandic as well, but the fog was making her uneasy. She just wanted to find a warm fire and a hot drink.

After all, pretty much everyone speaks English these days, don't they?

As she walked, her wheeled suitcase veering dangerously behind her on the uneven surface, the music got louder before it suddenly died altogether. Panic rose up inside Petra, and her pace quickened until a building loomed out of the mist ahead. She recognised only one word on the sign above the door, but it was the one that mattered – *krá*, Icelandic for pub.

This *krá* was much like the other Icelandic buildings she'd seen on the way from the airport: painted white, the clean colour and sharp lines contrasting sharply with the dark, jagged rock of the landscape. The roof of this building indicated that it had more than one storey, and Petra desperately hoped that this meant they had rooms to rent.

When she entered the bar, she half expected all conversations to stop as the occupants turned to stare at her. She imagined seeing the same thought written on all their faces: stupid foreigner.

But there were only a few people in the bar, and none of them gave her more than a cursory glance. There was an elderly couple, a man on his own staring morosely into his tankard, and a trio of what looked like young students.

The exterior of the building might have been stark and angular, but inside it was warm and welcoming. The wall behind the bar was covered with shelves, each groaning with dozens of different coloured bottles. As she approached, Petra wondered how many livers had failed as their owners tried to drink their way from top to bottom. The walls were painted a rich forest green with framed portraits and pictures of local landmarks on two of the walls and a well-used dartboard on the third.

Coming to a stop in front of the bar, she dug into her pocket for her small Icelandic guidebook and dictionary. It had been bought on a whim; she hadn't been planning on spending more time than was necessary driving from the airport to her client's warehouse and back again. Now, she was intensely grateful for her whimsy.

She tried to struggle her way through the phrase for "Do you have any rooms," but the barman merely scowled at her. Petra was frantically flicking through the book, looking for the phrase "My car has broken down" when a hand rested gently on her shoulder.

Petra turned to see one of the students – the girl – smiling at her with pity. 'Having trouble with the local language?'

Normally, Petra would have bridled at such a patronising tone from someone so much younger, but right now she needed all the help she could get. 'Yeah, a bit. My car broke down and I need a phone, or a bed, or both.'

The girl nodded then turned to the barman; out of her mouth came a series of guttural noises that sounded somehow fluid and beautiful. The barman shook his head and spoke in the same language, somehow not sounding quite as eloquent as the girl. 'He's sorry, but he has no rooms,' the girl said.

While the two were conversing, Petra had taken in her surroundings. Now she pointed at a wooden board behind the bar with the numbers one to six on it. There were hooks under each number, all empty except for number two.

'Can you ask him if that's where the room keys hang, please?'

The girl obliged, and the man glanced over his shoulder. Frowning, he said, '*Ja*,' that one word dripping with suspicion.

'Then tell him I'll take number two please,' Petra said, lightheaded with relief.

Even before the girl had finished translating, the barman leaned over and unhooked the key from its place. But instead of passing it to Petra, he placed it under the counter. He then spoke in a low, urgent voice.

Petra's interpreter looked uncomfortable. 'He says it's unlucky. He says that anyone who stays in that room never comes out again.'

Petra rolled her eyes. She'd heard about how landlords tried it on with obvious foreigners, attempting to drive their prices up by pretending scarcity. The thought of playing his greedy little game rankled, but she didn't have any choice. 'Look, ask him how much he usually charges for his rooms.' The girl did so then translated, and Petra dug deep into her wallet, bringing out double. She held it out to the landlord.

The man looked at it, his eyes sparkling with interest. Then he lowered his eyes and shook his head. Petra took some more *krona* out of her purse; double again.

The man looked longingly at the money then, to Petra's surprise, glanced at the girl. She looked over her shoulder at her two companions, and Petra felt a sudden electricity in the air. Then the girl nodded at the bartender who reluctantly took Petra's money; he handed over the key with even more reluctance.

'Thank you,' Petra said, feeling the tension between her shoulders unknot. Then, remembering her manners, she said, 'Þakka þér fyrir.' At least, she made an attempt at it; the man's scowl suggested that she'd failed spectacularly.

I wonder if I just told him I wanted to eat his dog or something.

'Come sit with us,' the girl said as the barman skulked off to get room two ready. Petra readily accepted.

As they were talking, the barman brought over a small glass of a green liquid that had a strange taste and burned all the way down. Petra learned from her new friends that it was called Brennivín, but she stopped them before they could tell her what was in it. She thought it best not to know.

He also brought her a pie which turned out to be fish in some kind of savoury sauce. It tasted peculiar to her European palette, but she still made short work of the meal.

Over the course of the next hour, she learned that her new companions were indeed exchange students as she had first thought. She also learned why the barman had been so reluctant to rent her room two.

'It's supposed to be filled with devils,' the boy named Jacob said. 'Legend says that any man who enters there never comes out. He's challenged to cards by the devils of hell, and he never wins.'

Petra shrugged. 'Well, that's okay because firstly I'm a woman, and secondly I can play cards with my eyes closed. I was the college champion at university.' She grinned at them; the girl, Mia, grinned back and the other boy, Felix, chuckled, but Jacob's face remained serious.

'You should not mock, madam, because all such rumours have a grain of truth to them, don't you find?'

Petra could think of several different counter-arguments, but it had been a strenuous day of travelling, not to mention the stress of her car breaking down; she wanted her bed, not a debate about rustic superstitions.

She stood up, drained her glass, then said to Jacob, 'Well, if you find me gone in the morning, you may inscribe on my headstone: "She should have listened to the stories," okay?'

Jacob glared at her, but Felix, who had been rooting around in his pockets, drew out a pack of cards. 'If you're such a card sharp, fancy playing a few hands with us before you go to bed? You can play with eyes open or closed, whatever you feel like.'

Petra glanced at her watch. A round of cards would be good fun. She regularly wiped the floor with the informal poker group she set up with some work colleagues; it had been ages since she'd played anyone new. The offer was very tempting.

But then she looked at Mia and Felix. They had open faces and friendly smiles, but their eyes were hard. A strong conviction rose in her mind that a game with them would not be quite as easy as she first imagined.

'That's kind, but I think I'll just go to bed,' she said, pushing her chair under the table.

Felix shrugged and offered her the cards. 'Well, take these anyway. You know, in case you meet any devils.' He glanced at Jacob who rolled his eyes. 'They're my lucky cards.'

Mia leaned forward and said in a stage whisper, 'He thinks because his name is Felix that he everything he touches is lucky.'

'Not everything,' Felix said, somewhat nettled. 'Just these cards.'

Petra found she couldn't take her eyes off the deck he was holding. Without any conscious instruction, her hand reached out and closed around the pack.

Felix quickly drew his hand back. 'Goodnight then, Petra, and good luck.'

Tucking the pack into her pocket with an air

of embarrassment, Petra said goodnight, then went to the bar and held up her key, the universal sign for "show me to my room, good sir."

The barman grunted and headed through a low door in the far corner. Petra followed him up a set of stairs which were so ancient and brittle that she was amazed when she reached the top without her foot going through at least one of them.

Her room was shabby but clean. The bedsheets were fresh and the mattress reasonably comfortable. She stripped off, had a wash, then got dressed again; it was far too cold to sleep in pyjamas. Fully dressed, she climbed into bed but found she wasn't sleepy. She took Felix's cards out of her pocket and flicked through them. The deck had the familiar four suits, but the picture cards were strangely archaic. They had representations of angels on them rather than kings, queens, and jacks. She put them back in the packet and folded her hands over her chest, the cards beneath them. Staring up at the ceiling, she fervently hoped that tomorrow would be better.

I'm not meeting Gunnar until tomorrow afternoon. And I was going to stay in a hotel in

Strandakirkja tonight anyway, so I'm not really that far off track staying here instead. I'll just have a longer journey tomorrow, that's all.

With that comforting thought in her mind, she slipped into sleep.

~

Petra awoke to darkness and a strange bed; it took her a moment to remember where she was. Aching all over, she lifted her hand to look at her watch. The electronic face read 11:11. The numbers looked somehow sinister, lined up all the same like that.

'You're awake then,' a voice said from the corner of her room.

Petra scrambled to her feet. Realising that she still held the cards, she tightened her grip and drew her arm back, ready to throw them at this intruder.

A lamp on the small table by the wall was switched on. Petra saw that an old man was sitting there. He was scrawny and his beard was matted. Every dirty line of his face was etched with utter exhaustion, although his voice had been level enough. On his lap was a hessian sack, which he clutched tightly.

She relaxed slightly; she could probably take him in a fight.

'Who are you? What are you doing in my room?'

The man frowned. 'I can't remember my name. They just call me the soldier now,' he looked down at his grimy uniform, 'although I haven't fought alongside a brother soldier in such a long time.'

'Do you need money?' Petra lowered her arm although her heart was still hammering.

He looked at her with bloodshot eyes. 'What I need is rest, and release.'

Not in my bloody room, you don't.

'I can give you a few *króna* for a room.'

He shook his head. 'Money means nothing to me now. I used to be rich, have a wife, a son. But they're gone. It's just me,' his face darkened, 'and Him.'

Petra felt gooseflesh crawl across her skin. 'Him?'

He sighed. 'I am truly sorry. I have to feed him or he will die. Then he'll be reborn in Hell, and he'll send his creatures after me. They'll tear me limb from limb and...' His voice cut off with a sob.

'Look, mate, I'm just here on a work trip. Let me give you some money and—'

The soldier held up the grubby sack. 'Do you know what this is?'

'Yes.'

'Well, what is it?' he said irritably.

'A sack.'

'If it's a sack, then get in it.'

A hot, dry wind raced around Petra, and she threw her hands up to protect her face from its scorching heat. Stumbling backwards, her foot met empty air, and then she was falling. She screamed, waving her arms in the desperate hope of a handhold, bracing herself for the inevitable impact. But she just kept falling.

Oh god, there was a hole in the floor. I'm going to crash through into the bar below and break my back and never walk again and—

She landed on something soft yet spiky which bent under her, breaking her fall but leaving her winded. Rolling onto her side, she felt grass beneath her cheek.

The window. I must have fallen out of the window, onto a bush or something. Yet around her was not the barren landscape of Iceland, but grass plains rolling away to woods and hills.

Shocked, she sat up. Above her, the sky wasn't the bright blue of day or the deep indigo of night; instead, it was a brownish colour with small lights that were too regularly spaced to be stars. An oppressive gloom hung over this strange land.

Like the inside of a— She cut off that thought abruptly. It was ridiculous, not to mention impossible.

A gust of foul air wafted over her from behind. She turned and saw a cave which had been gouged out of the side of a small rocky hill. Out of the darkness came a melodious voice.

'Ah. Fresh meat. Welcome.'

Petra scrambled up and backed away. 'Who are you? What are you doing in that cave?'

'I'm in the shadows, where your kind put me.'

'Show yourself.'

There was a soft chuckle. 'You wouldn't want to see me. Not the real me.'

Fear twisted Petra's stomach, sending spasms of pain to her rapidly beating heart. 'What is this place?' she called out, her voice wavering slightly

'It's the world I have created.'

'Created? Just who the hell are you?'

There was a soft chuckle. 'Who the hell indeed. Didn't he tell you? I'm the Devil.'

'The Devil doesn't exist,' she said flatly. Part of her was aware it was an automatic response, one without much thought in it and which, crucially, didn't take current circumstances into account.

A sigh came from the cave. 'Do I have to show myself to prove my own existence? How tiring.'

Petra backed away further. 'No, don't, I— Oh.'

A man, not a monster, had stepped from the cave. He was a little taller than her with sandy-coloured hair, blue eyes, and a mischievous smile that looked as if it never left his lips. He wore a jacket and trouser suit that was in decent condition, if a little dated. His shoes were black and highly polished.

He made a gesture that encompassed his body. 'It's not my true form, obviously. But it'll do for now. I wouldn't want to scare you. I like to have some conversation before I dine. Conversation is so rare here.'

'Look, I'm not a meal.' Petra glanced behind her, wondering how far and how fast she could run. When she turned back, the man was standing immediately before her. He'd covered the distance soundlessly and impossibly fast.

'Don't worry. I'll make it fast. That's what your kind forgets about me. I have both mercy and justice in my dealings. You're a good woman, I can tell. I wouldn't want you to suffer. But I have to eat. I'm so hungry.' A blackness shimmered over his irises then, turning his eyes pure ebony for one terrible moment.

'Don't eat me!' Petra said, her voice high and quavering. He gave her a pitying look.

Pull yourself together, you stupid bitch.

She thought fast. 'That man – the soldier – he told me if you didn't eat then you'd die and go back to Hell. Wouldn't that free you?'

He frowned at her. 'Is that what he said? It's possible, I suppose. If I die on Earth, my soul flies straight back to my realm. But this sack was crafted with a magic beyond my knowledge. Who knows what would happen if I died in here.'

Petra looked up at the brown sky. 'We're really in a sack?' When she thought about it, those strange, regular dots could be light creeping through a hessian weave.

'Yes. The world used to be full of wonders. They're rare these days, or so I understand from those he sends me, but this sack still exists. It's a bitter irony, I must say.

'This sack was created by The Other Side, that's why I can't escape from it. I can't be sure if my soul would be able to escape if it perished in here, so I'd rather just eat you and bide my time, I'm afraid. But it was a nice idea.'

He stepped forward and she threw her hands up to ward him off. A look of astonishment lit up his face. 'Is that a pack of cards?'

Taken aback, Petra realised she was still holding them. 'Yes.'

'Oh, I haven't paid cards in such a long time.' There was a longing in his voice, almost as sharp as the hunger in his eyes.

Petra seized this chance of an extended life. 'I'll play with you, if you like.'

His face briefly contorted with indecision. 'Very well. A few hands then, before dinner. What will the stakes be?'

'If I win, you don't eat me.'

He sighed. 'I cannot agree to that. I am most terribly sorry.'

'Okay then, not that,' she said hurriedly. 'How about, if I win, you don't eat me long enough to listen to my proposal to escape?'

'You could just tell me now.'

'I haven't thought of it yet. But I will,' she said quickly. 'That's what I do. I create solutions for impossible situations.'

His laugh came all the way from his empty belly and echoed around their prison. 'Oh, I do like a woman with fire and hope. He hasn't sent me one of those for so long. But those are the stakes if you win – what if *I* win? You've nothing to offer me.'

She considered this. 'True, but you'll have had the pleasure of playing cards. Even without proper stakes, wouldn't it be worth it? How long has it been since you've done anything except talk and eat?'

'Far too long,' he said morosely. 'Very well. Best of a hundred and one hands then? I can wait a couple of hours.'

Petra felt giddy with relief. *But all I've bought is a little extra time. I still need to use it to think of a way out of here.*

'Where shall we play?' she asked.

'Right here,' he said, indicating an empty patch of grass that instantly burst apart as a stone table and two elegant chairs rose up. When it was fully revealed and the echoes of its birthing had died away, the Devil brushed a few stray lumps of soil from it and sat in one of the chairs. Petra took the other one.

'There are no chips,' she commented.

'Oh, my sincere apologies.' The ground next to the table rumbled and a sapling shot forth; in a few seconds, it was a mature oak tree. Leaf buds burst all along the branches. The leaves quickly turned from spring green to emerald and then the colours of autumn, at which point they drifted down into two neat piles, one beside the Devil and one by Petra

'Two hundred each should see us a good start,' the Devil said.

'That was... impressive.'

'Thank you. I can only work with the materials I have.'

'Really? So how come there's grass and stone and trees inside a... sack?' The impossibility of it all threatened to overwhelm her for a moment: trapped in a sack playing cards with the Devil.

But an Architect deals with what is, not what should be.

The Devil shuffled the cards as he explained. 'One man came in with grass on his feet, so I used that to make the rolling plains. A woman was sent clutching a bunch of flowers so I made those. Look closely and you will note that there are only four species growing here – the four that she brought with her. And a child was transported in here while playing a game with stones, so I could create my cave.'

Petra froze. 'He sent you *a child?*'

The Devil dealt the cards then looked at her levelly. 'Yes.'

'He's a monster,' Petra whispered.

'Is he?' the Devil said idly as he examined his hand. 'Many would say it's a good thing to keep the Prince of Darkness from the world.' He glanced up then, and his eyes were completely black. 'However, *I'd* say that he's a miserable bastard, and as soon as I get out of here, I'm going to rip him limb from limb, gorge myself on his blood, sate myself on his flesh, and suck his marrow dry. Then I'll give him life and do it all over again.'

Despite the dryness of her mouth, Petra said, 'Like Prometheus.'

The Devil beamed. 'How delightful that there's still some worthwhile education in the world and the old tales aren't forgotten.'

'Some tales are, like those about magic sacks,'

she added ruefully, gazing at the hessian sky once again.

'Shall we play?'

'Yes.' Petra studied her cards then glanced at the table. Playing cards *and* thinking of a way to save her own life; it was going to be a challenging couple of hours.

~

Petra spent the first thirty hands learning her opponent's tells and habits. The Devil was a tricky man to read, but not impossible, possibly because he hadn't played for so long. When she was comfortably in the lead, she set part of her mind to solving the puzzle of how to get out of there. The answer was frustratingly elusive.

As the Devil frowned over his fiftieth hand, she looked around the world he had created. *If I actually get out of here, no one is going to believe that I was in a sack playing cards with the Devil. No one would believe it unless they were here and saw it with their own eyes...* The back of her neck prickled, just as it always did when a possible solution was taking hold of her mind. She examined the idea, started to build it up in her head.

Petra's mind was so engrossed that she lost

the next three hands. She concentrated harder on the game. There was no point in having a solution to this mess if she lost her chance to share it before he killed her.

When the one hundred and first hand was complete, Petra stared at the two piles of leaves. It was a close thing, but her heap was just a little larger.

'Interesting cards you have,' the Devil commented. 'Where did you get them?'

'Some kids in the *krá* gave them to me.'

'*Krá*? We're in Iceland then?'

'Yes. Didn't you know?'

He shrugged. 'I've seen only the inside of a sack for several centuries.' He looked at her thoughtfully. 'These kids – good looking, were they?'

'Yes. I suppose so. Why?'

The Devil shrugged then asked, 'So, what's your plan then?'

Petra's heart jolted. The plan she'd come up with was shaky, but it was the best she had.

'Well, I want to get out, and so do you, right?'

'Very astute.'

'But we can't while he's guarding the sack.'

'No.'

'So, we need to get him to give it to someone else, someone who will let us out.'

'He'll never give it up. Even if he did, who would let the Devil out into the world?'

'I would.'

The Devil raised his eyebrow. 'But you're in here.'

'Is there any way that *I* can get out?'

'Couldn't tell you, not my magic.'

Petra considered this. 'What were the words I said to get sucked in here?'

'I believe the formula is that he says "what is this?" then you reply with "it's a sack," and he says "well, if this is a sack then get in it."'

'What would happen if I spoke his part and he spoke mine? Would that reverse our positions?'

The Devil looked thoughtful. 'It might. I can't say for sure, although it makes the sort of sense you get with magic. But how do you plan on tricking him into saying those words?'

Petra smiled. 'Oh, I don't plan to trick him. I plan to make him *want* to change places.'

The Devil looked at her, astounded, then laughed. 'Now *that* I'd like to see.'

~

Even though it was an illusion, Petra couldn't help but luxuriate in how wonderful the silken gown felt. She always wore real silk pants for important meetings, and right now she was intensely glad of it. The dress was a pale cream with intricate stitching on the bodice. It was tight around the waist and bust but loose and flowing past her hips.

The Devil had also used the silk from her pants to create a great bell tent, supported by wire from her underwired bra. Her plain cotton shirt had been used as the basis for the celebratory pennants that hung from all the trees. At the base of the trees were piles of gold that the Devil had made from her bracelet and earrings. The stone table was covered with rich food; there was no substance to it, every morsel was pure illusion.

Using wood from the trees and hair from her head, he'd also created some rudimentary instruments that played themselves. They looked ungainly, but the music they gave off was sweet enough.

Perhaps the crowning achievement was the angels he'd made from the cards.

'Now,' the Devil said, sweat beading his brow,

'I suggest you laugh and dance as if your life depended on it – which it does.'

Petra smiled and mingled with the cardboard angels who spoke a language she couldn't understand.

The Devil lounged under one of the trees.

'Aren't you joining in?' Petra called out, trying to keep her voice light.

'It took a lot of magic to create this celebration and even more to keep it going. I need to rest and preserve my strength. If your plan fails, I will have to devour you in a matter of moments just to stay alive.'

'It *will* work,' Petra said, her fixed smile making her cheeks ache.

The sky parted and bright light flooded in for a moment until the old soldier's face blocked it out. He peered down at her, his head filling the sky, his eyes narrowed.

'What is this noise?'

The Devil threw his arms wide. 'Oh, thank you, old man, thank you!'

The soldier looked startled. 'Thank you? Why?'

'You've kept me in this sack for so long that Heaven tells me that the penance for my rebellion is over and I am redeemed. Of course, they cannot let me back into Heaven, but they have granted me the next best thing.'

'Which is?'

The Devil beamed and gestured around. 'Why, Heaven on Earth! Well, in this sack anyway. They sent this young girl to tell me so.'

Petra tried to keep her smile steady as she gave a little wave.

Take the bait, please, please.

The soldier's old face creased into a frown. 'It seems unfair that *she* should get the joy of being in a corner of Heaven when she hasn't done anything. After all, it was me who kept you in this sack all those years.'

'It was indeed,' the Devil replied, his teeth gritted.

'It isn't fair. It should be me in there reaping the rewards of your redemption.'

The Devil shrugged. 'I couldn't agree more. But unless you can swap places with her, she's here now, and that's that.'

Petra threw herself to her knees, gripping the Devil's coat. 'No! Please don't cast me out! The angels told me I could stay. They said it would be my reward.'

'Reward?' snapped the soldier. 'What have you done, woman? I have wandered for years, outcast and alone. I should be in there, not you.' The passion behind his words sent spit flying into their world, globules as large as hailstones. He looked beseechingly at the Devil. 'How do I swap places with her?'

The Devil took a moment, as if thinking it through. 'I suppose you could get her to say the words you normally say, and vice versa.'

'Yes!' cried the soldier. He looked at Petra. 'Say "Do you know what this is?"'

Petra folded her arms. 'I will *not*.'

The soldier appealed to the Devil. 'Help me. After all, you would not be redeemed if not for me.'

'I suppose I do owe you a great debt,' the Devil replied, an edge to his voice.

He picked Petra up by the neck, his fingers digging into her throat, almost choking her.

'Say the words,' he snarled. His eyes were black again.

'I—'

'Say them!'

From the corner of her eye, she could see the paper angels starting to come apart and the strings on the musical instruments beginning to break.

She looked up at the great visage in the sky and, in a croaky voice, said, 'Do you know what this is?'

'It's a sack!' cried the soldier in triumph.

'If it's a sack, then get in it.'

Instantly, the hands were ripped from her throat and she was falling backwards again. She landed, hard, on wooden floorboards that grazed her hands and knees. Breathing hard, she looked around and found herself back in her Icelandic hotel room. On the floor lay the sack, writhing and twitching. She dived for it, pulling the cords tight around the top. The sack jerked so violently that it pulled itself out of her hands and went rolling across the floor. There were screams and snarls from inside, then a sickening crunch before the bag went silent and still. Petra clamped her hand over her mouth, holding back the urge to vomit as a dark red stain leaked from the sack onto the floor.

The room was dimly lit by just a single lamp, and it took some moments for Petra to realise that it was growing darker still. She stared around and saw grotesque shapes crawling down the walls. Hideous forms were sneaking through the shadows, advancing towards her and the bag.

'Your promise,' came a whisper. 'Your promissssss—'

There were three loud knocks on the door. The dark shapes skittered away, leaving empty shadows in their wake. Petra knelt motionless until the knocks came again. She got up on trembling legs and staggered to the door. Her hands were shaking so much she nearly couldn't open it.

Outside were the three exchange students – only now, as they stood before her, Petra wondered how she could have possibly thought them teenagers. They were old, she saw, older than the soldier, but young as well. She rubbed her eyes, certain that they had to be one thing or the other, but still all she saw was a very beautiful, extremely old trio of...

Felix grinned. 'You won, then? Glad my cards were lucky for you.'

'Did you know that was going to happen?' Petra asked, uncertain whether to be angry or scared. Had they set her up or saved her?

Felix shrugged. 'It was a distinct possibility.'

Mia held out her hand. 'May I have the sack, please?'

Petra pulled the door towards her, blocking their way inside. 'Why? What do you want it for?'

'For safekeeping,' Jacob said sourly.

Petra glanced round at the sack in its spreading pool of blood. A rush of warm air, scented with honey, brushed past her face. When she turned back, the corridor was empty. Instead, the three figures were inside the room, standing around the sack, looking down at it. Mia picked it up, grimacing at the dripping blood.

'I'm not sure you should have that,' Petra said, starting towards them.

Felix took a step forward, positioning himself between Petra and Mia – between Petra and the sack. 'Would you rather the Other Side came for it?' He glanced at the walls. 'I believe we heard them come a-calling just before we knocked.'

A shudder went down Petra's spine. Felix smiled. 'I didn't think so.'

They moved past her to the door. They were halfway out when she called after them, 'What happens to those who break a deal with the Devil?'

'They die in terrible agony before their time,' Felix said with that same easy smile he always wore.

'Unless,' Mia added, 'He never finds them, of course.' She shook the sack, and Petra felt sure that she heard a distant squeal of rage. Mia smiled at her. 'We shall all hope for that outcome.' Then there was another rush of sweet air, and the corridor was empty.

A Wolf in the House

'Your father is going to take you to the fair today, sweetheart. Won't that be nice?'

Purdey looked up from her breakfast, her shoulders tensing. 'But... I was going to go with my friends.'

Isaac lowered his spoon into his porridge bowl. 'What's this? Too old to be going out with me, your own pa?'

You're not my Pa. He died seven winters ago. You're just Ma's husband.

Purdey's eyes flicked between her mother and stepfather. 'But all my friends are going. We were going to get our fortunes told.'

'Tell you what, why not come with me, then you can join your friends later?' Isaac's tone might have been light, but his eyes glittered dangerously.

Purdey realised she had no choice in this. 'Yes, Pa,' she said quietly. That single word left such a tight lump in her throat that she struggled to swallow her food.

At that moment, Purdey's little half-sister, Tressa, came bounding in. She went immediately to her father and hugged him tightly. 'Guess what, little starfish,' he whispered in her ear, 'I'm taking my girls to the fair today.'

Tressa gave off a high-pitched shriek of excitement that had Isaac wincing and rubbing his ear.

'If you don't deafen your old pa first, that is. Now, get on and eat your breakfast, or you'll be hungry before we get there.'

Purdey considered dawdling over her porridge to delay the inevitable, but she knew that Tressa would be bouncing with excitement, and slowness would irritate her stepfather. So she ate, washed, and combed her hair in good time before going to get their cloaks from the hooks by the door.

She took down Tressa's best cloak, a dark green one with little flowers stitched around the hood, and selected the cloak that she wore to school every fourth day. She nearly dropped them when she discovered Isaac standing behind her.

He eyed her school cloak and said, 'What about the red one I bought you?'

Purdey's mouth opened then closed. She couldn't tell him that she hated it. As his brows furrowed together, she blurted out, 'I didn't want to get it dirty.'

His frown cleared, but his lips were still pressed together. 'It's good that you think of such things, but I didn't spend a whole silver penny on that cloak for it to sit idle on the stand. Wear it today.'

With great reluctance, Purdey took down the red cloak. It was made of the finest wool and dyed the colour of summer roses. All her friends had cooed over it when her mother had made her wear it to school. But the feel of it against her, even through her clothes, made Purdey shudder. If she was honest, she thought it a thing of beauty; it had been the gleam in Isaac's eyes as he had laid it around her shoulders that had ruined the gift for her.

Once she had fastened it, Isaac nodded approvingly. He glanced round then said in a low voice, 'That colour suits you. You look like a proper woman wearing that.'

Purdey's heart jolted, and she walked quickly past him to take Tressa her cloak. When she felt him reach out and brush the edge of her cloak as she passed, she had to hold back a shudder.

~

Despite Purdey's discomfort at being forced to go to the fair with her stepfather and half-sister, excitement started to grow inside her as they approached the village. On the breeze, the sweetness of honeyed almonds mingled with the tantalising aroma of meat on a griddle.

'I want to do it all!' Tressa squealed as they approached the first lot of stalls set up in the sprawling space outside the village walls.

Her father chuckled indulgently. 'We'll do as much as my purse allows, sweet one.'

Purdey slipped her hand into her pocket. She had five copper pennies in there that she'd saved from selling her hens' eggs at market and running errands for some of the farmers. Neither her mother nor Isaac knew about the money; she didn't think they'd take it from her, but it had felt important that she have her own hidden stash.

Tressa wanted to have a go at the archery and burst into tears when told she wasn't strong enough. Isaac placated her by saying that she could try with him. It was a sweet sight, seeing him kneel next to Tressa, wrapping his arms around her so that they could pull the bowstring back together.

Purdey looked around; while the other stalls were interesting, she couldn't see the fortune teller's tent. She'd been too shy to go in last year, but this year, she was determined to go in with her friends, Wenna and Esolde.

As Isaac and Tressa left the archery butts, Trengrouse the baker stepped away from his stall selling sweet buns and approached them. He shook hands with Isaac, flour dusting the ground beneath them, then cooed over Tressa who drank up the attention.

As he turned to Purdey, he said, 'Well, Isaac, look at your little stepdaughter. Hasn't she grown?'

'Indeed, she has. Quite the little woman now.' Isaac rested his hand on her shoulder. Her skin itched with the heat of him.

'You shall have to be watching her, what with all the young boys around, aye?' Trengrouse said with a wink.

Isaac's grip didn't increase, but she felt his hand go rigid. In a calm, cold voice, he said, 'Those young boys had better watch their step where my pretty Purdey is concerned.'

Trengrouse's good-humour faltered. 'But of course, of course! I didn't mean anything by it. Here, lass,' he added, crossing back to his stall then returning with a sweet bun in each hand, 'have a bun. No, Isaac, no charge,' he said, waving away the coin as he gave one to Tressa as well. 'Just a little present. Got a girl of my own. We fathers have to watch out for our daughters, don't we?'

'That we do,' Isaac agreed.

As they wandered through the rest of the fair, Purdey nibbled on her bun while Tressa devoured hers in obscenely big mouthfuls. Isaac stopped at a tent where several men were sitting at tables playing knucklebones. A young woman wandered between them, taking coin and filling up their tankards.

Tressa sidled over to Purdey and looked up, the picture of innocence. 'Nice bun?'

Purdey narrowed her eyes. 'Yes, it is. I'm really enjoying mine.'

Tressa's face fell slightly. Then it brightened as she added, 'But they were very big, weren't they? You probably couldn't manage to eat *all* of it.'

'If you could eat yours, little shrimp, I'm sure I can.'

Tressa pouted. 'I'm *not* a shrimp.'

'Yes, you are. Here you go, shrimp,' she said, handing over the last quarter of her bun, 'eat this and see if you can grow into a lobster.'

Tressa beamed then hugged Purdey tightly, leaving sticky fingerprints on the red cloak. 'You're the best sister.'

'Don't be so sure, because if you do turn into a lobster, I'm going to give you to Ma for the pot. Come here, little lobster.'

Tressa squeaked in surprise and delight as her sister lunged for her and missed. Purdey chased her round for a while before collapsing on the floor. Tressa immediately climbed onto her lap and ate the rest of her bun.

At that moment, Purdey could almost imagine that she was happy. She closed her eyes, enjoying the spring warmth, so welcome after the chill winter. A shadow fell over her and she shivered. Opening her eyes, she saw her stepfather standing over them.

Isaac smiled tenderly. 'Look at my two girls getting on so well.'

'Purdey gave me her bun!' Tressa said, holding her sticky fingers up as proof.

Before Isaac could comment, Purdey's two friends raced up. Purdey scrambled to her feet, dislodging Tressa who squeaked indignantly.

Esolde grabbed her hand and said, 'Oh, Purdey! You have to come see the hoopla! It's such fun. I want the little bracelet they have.'

Wenna tossed her head, her red curls flashing in the sun. 'You never get any of the prizes from these stalls.'

'Young Tom not with you?' Isaac asked. 'Nor that little lad, what's he called? Simon?'

'No, sir,' said Wenna in that careful, respectful voice she only ever used with grownups. 'Tom has been sentenced to do chores, and Simon has the itching pox.' Folding her hands before her, she said politely, 'Please can Purdey come with us, sir? To have her fortune told?'

Isaac chuckled. 'How could I resist a request

from such a little angel?' He reached out and tickled her under the chin. Wenna gave a little squeal of pleasure and ducked back, grinning.

'Alright then, be off you three. Stay out of trouble and away from the boys. And Purdey,' Isaac said, staring at her meaningfully, 'I want you back by the fifth bell so we can all walk back together – understand?'

'Yes, Pa.'

'And before I forget, here's a copper penny each.' Wenna and Esolde took the offered money eagerly, their mouths filled with profuse thanks. Purdey took hers reluctantly, her thanks little more than a whisper.

'Your stepfather is so generous,' Esolde said as they walked away.

'And so handsome,' Wenna added with a grin.

Esolde looked scandalised. 'You can't think of him that way! He's her pa.'

'He's not my pa,' Purdey said through gritted teeth.

'See?' said Wenna triumphantly.

'He's still Tressa's pa though,' Purdey shot back.

Wenna shrugged. 'All men are somebody's father eventually. I like his shoulders, and his beard – it's so neat. Not like that caterpillar hair that Jory is trying to grow.' She and Esolde dissolved into giggles. Even Purdey smiled. Jory's woeful attempts to grow a beard were the talk of the schoolroom.

They came to a tent with an impressive board outside that proclaimed, amid stars and swirls, "Lady Morven, Daughter of the Sea, Founder of the Rocks, Seer of Ages."

'You first,' said Wenna, pushing Esolde forward. Protesting, but giggling, Esolde led them into the tent. It was hot and murky inside, the air smelling strongly of something that was both spicy and floral. There was a round table on which a single black candle burned with a pale blue flame.

'Who comes seeking wisdom?' The voice must have come from the other side of the tent, yet it sounded as if it came from very far away. For the briefest of moments, Purdey was convinced that the tent stretched out for miles.

Then a figure limped into the glow of the candlelight. The woman's full lips and bright eyes suggested she'd been beautiful once. But now her face was lined, her black hair was mixed with grey, and her shoulders were hunched.

'We do,' said Wenna boldly. 'Esolde would like her fortune told, wouldn't you?' She gave her friend a shove, and Esolde almost careered into the table.

'Very well,' said Lady Morven irritably. 'Sit.'

With a nervous look over her shoulder, Esolde sat down in front of the rickety table. Morven slumped down on the other side and demanded, 'Palm.'

Esolde obediently held out her hand, and Morven seized it, bringing it close to her face. Then she lowered it gently onto the table, leaned back, and closed her eyes. Purdey and Wenna exchanged amused glances, then Morven spoke in a deep, sonorous voice that wasn't at all humorous. 'You will obtain a small fortune from an unexpected place, but you will learn one thing that is more valuable than all gold. Beware cats and look before you step into puddles.'

She opened her eyes and looked a little dazed. A sharp shudder seemed to bring her back to herself. Glaring at Esolde, she held her hand out and snapped, 'Payment.'

Esolde quickly obliged then stood up, looking a little shaken. 'I've always hated cats,' she whispered to Purdey as Wenna took her seat.

Morven glared at the girl. 'I shall ask *you* for payment first.'

Grumbling, Wenna dug out her coin and handed it over. The same ritual was repeated, and the fortune pronounced this time was, 'You will fall in love once and be broken-hearted by the next full moon. But one friend will be thought false and proven true, if you take care to watch the harvest.'

Wenna stood up, looking affronted. 'Broken-hearted indeed,' she muttered as Purdey took a seat.

Purdey obediently held out her hand. Morven stared at her through narrowed eyes. It occurred to Purdey that maybe she needed to pay Morven first, as Wenna had done. But she found herself pinned by that gaze.

Morven sniffed. 'That is a fine cloak you wear.'

'Yes,' said Purdey uncomfortably. 'My stepfather bought it for me.'

'Expensive too. But you don't like it.'

'No.' The admission was out before she could stop it. She glanced guiltily over her shoulder at Wenna and Esolde, but the two girls were staring into the distance.

'Don't worry about them,' Morven said. 'They are lost in their own thoughts. They will find their way back soon enough. But I do not think I should tell your future, pretty Purdey.' Her skin prickled as if ants crawled over it. 'That's what he calls you, isn't it?'

'Yes.' She summoned up a hot anger to chase away the cold fear inside her. 'But I thought you were supposed to tell my future, not my present. Why can't you tell me about a fortune, or some good luck, or a handsome prince to...?' She faltered, feeling suddenly foolish.

'To take you away?' Morven spat and shook her head. 'I cannot predict such trite rubbish.' She leaned forward, her voice lowered. 'But I can predict that if you go to the standing stone when the moon is high tonight, you will meet someone who can help you.'

'Who? My parents will strangle me if I try to go out that late.'

'Here.' Morven reached into a pouch at her waist and handed over a phial with a small amount of clear liquid in it. 'Tip this into your mother's stew, and they should all sleep soundly. Make sure you have blackberry seeds in your teeth so that it won't take you the same way.'

Purdey stared at the bottle. 'What's in it?'
Morven merely grinned. Irritated, Purdey said,
'Well, what if we're not having stew tonight?
What should I put it in?'

'You *are* having stew tonight. There, you see,'
Morven said triumphantly, 'I foretold your
future. Now,' she slammed her hand on the
table, eliciting two small gasps from behind
Purdey, 'out, you silly girls. Make way for all the
noble lords and ladies who come seeking
Morven's wisdom.'

Purdey stood up and found that her two
friends were already hurrying out of the tent.
She followed them, squinting at the brightness
outside.

'What did Lady Morven say to you?' Esolde
asked as they wandered between the stalls.

Purdey thought of the fortune teller's strange
advice then said, 'That I was having stew tonight.'

Esolde and Wenna exchanged glances then
burst into laughter. 'I'd ask for your ha'penny
back,' said Esolde.

Purdey found a smile from somewhere, but
she was too distracted to join in fully. The phial
in her pocket felt heavier than a whole purse of
coins.

Should I really put it in their stew? What if it hurts Ma or Tressa? I wouldn't want anything to happen to them. But if it were to do something to Isaac...

Purdey tried to put such wonderings out of her mind. The fair would only be here today and tomorrow, so this might be her only chance to have some fun.

The three of them pooled their remaining money and had enough for an enjoyable afternoon. They had a go at the horseshoes, winning a glass of mead that they shared between them. There was bobbing for apples run by a young man who winked at them when they approached. Esolde tried, but Wenna declared that the apples were too wrinkled to bother with, and Purdey had to agree. They watched some of the older boys from school throwing a hammer at a target, laughing when one of the oldest nearly dropped the hammer on his own foot.

They didn't have quite enough coins to afford some of the griddled meat being served up on dark brown trenchers, but they did have sufficient to have several goes with the skittles. They ended up laughing merrily all afternoon.

By the time the fifth bell rang, Purdey was at

her appointed meeting spot and ready to go home. Tressa was so weary that Isaac carried her, and she fell asleep almost instantly on his shoulder. He walked ahead and Purdey hung back, taking the opportunity to grab a blackberry and stuff it in her mouth. She sucked away all the juice until only the husk and the seeds remained, and she wedged them in the side of her cheek.

When they came home, her mother was sitting at the table. She stood up and kissed her husband. Then, leaning back and giving him a coquettish smile as she said, 'Please, sir, I've done all my chores – may *I* go to the fair tomorrow?'

'What do you think I am, Margaret, made of money?' he snapped, pushing her away. He placed Tressa on her seat where she blearily rubbed her eyes. Then he turned back to his wife and asked in a cold voice, 'Or do you want to go there and act like a slut in front of all the men?'

White-faced, Margaret said, 'No, I just—'

'I know your game. All women play it, always at the expense of us men.' He rolled his shoulders and seemed to ease some of the tension out of his body. 'Still, be a good wife tonight, and fulfil all your duties, and we'll see what the morning brings.'

'Yes, Isaac, of course,' Margaret said meekly.

Purdey saw the look that passed between them before her mother turned away. She knew that there were wifely duties that were only to be done in the dark, although she wasn't quite certain what they were. Wenna had told her some shocking stories, but Purdey didn't know whether to believe them or not.

As her mother went to set the table, Isaac turned to his stepdaughter. For a moment, he still wore the same look that he'd worn for his wife, and Purdey felt as if someone had filled her stomach with snow. Then the look was gone, and he smiled at her. 'Did you have fun with your friends today, pretty Purdey?'

'Yes. Thank you.'

He looked down at Tressa and beamed. 'And did you have fun with your Papa, little one?'

'Again, again!' Tressa said. 'Tomorrow, tomorrow!'

Isaac chuckled. 'We'll see, little starfish.'

Morven had been correct; Purdey's mother had made stew for dinner. While Isaac was unlacing his boots and Tressa was washing her sticky face, Purdey offered to stir the pot while her mother set the table. With her back to the room, Purdey chose her moment to tip the contents of the bottle into the pan.

After dinner, everyone curled up around the fire. Margaret sewed, Tressa played with her doll, and Purdey practised her handwriting for school next week. Isaac dozed in front of the fire until his wife drowsily announced it was time for bed. It seemed to Purdey that everyone, except for her, was falling asleep as they walked. Nevertheless, she waited a whole chiming hour after the candle went out before she slipped out of the house.

~

It wasn't far from Purdey's cottage to the standing stone which rested halfway up a hill. The night was lit by a brilliant full moon and the journey was easy enough. However, she kept glancing over her shoulder at the empty path, sure that someone was following her.

The standing stone stood just above a small wood that covered the bottom of the hill. As Purdey reached the tree-line, she hesitated. It was dark under the trees, but looking ahead at the expanse of hillside she'd have to cross made her feel very exposed.

As she contemplated her choices, a wolf howl rang out through the night. Purdey cringed back into the shadows. The howl came again, from just the other side of the hill, and closer.

While she stood uncertain whether to hide or flee, she saw a young man walk around the stone. He slicked back his shoulder-length hair and adjusted his jerkin. Then he looked straight at her, even though Purdey could have sworn she must be invisible amongst the trees.

'Halloo there,' he called out in a friendly voice. 'Were you looking for someone?'

He might be a stranger, but right now he represented an element of safety that the dark night was lacking. Purdey hurried towards him and said urgently, 'I heard a wolf.'

'I'm sure.' He seemed completely unconcerned.

'Are we safe here?'

'Well, I am.'

His reply unsettled her. 'Who are you? Have we met?'

'I'm Branok. I work at the fair.'

In a flash, she had placed him: the lad

running the apple bobbing who had winked at them. 'Really? Morven said you could help me.'

'That depends. Are you pretty Purdey?'

She flinched. 'Don't call me that. But yes, I'm Purdey.'

He bowed. 'Then I can help you, if you help me in return.'

Cold dread seeped through her. How could she have been so stupid as to think someone would help her for nothing? 'Help you? How?'

'By opening the door to your parents' cottage.'

She narrowed her eyes. 'Do you want to steal from us? Is that it?'

His gaze fell to her hands. 'Your fingers are stained with ink, like you've been writing or reading. Do you go to school?'

'Yes, we all do around here. It's a very well-thought-of place,' she said defensively. Purdey was beginning to regret coming.

'I didn't go to school, so I never learned to read, but I bet I know something you don't know.'

'And what's that?'

'That men can turn into wolves.'

His reply startled her. Then she thought of

the howl, the memory of how it had chilled her blood still fresh in her mind. 'That's just a fairy story. No man can do that.'

He cocked his head. 'Is that so?'

He turned and strolled behind the stone, out of sight. Purdey was looking around anxiously when there was a low, agonised groan that turned into a bestial snarl. A moment later, a slender brown wolf trotted out from behind the stone.

Purdey shrieked then turned and ran. But it was a hopeless contest; she'd barely taken five steps before the creature had crashed into her, sending her tumbling to the ground. She twisted, trying to roll away, but the beast placed its front paws on her chest, pinning her in place. For a long, long moment, she stared up into hungry golden eyes and felt sure it was Death looking down at her.

Then, to her shock, the wolf moved away, trotting back behind the stone. A moment later, Branok reappeared, smoothing down his hair and adjusting his jerkin once more.

He leaned against the stone and grinned at her. 'There. Now you can tell your friends at school you know something they don't.'

Purdey scrambled to her feet, shaking all over. 'What are you?'

'I've been called many names. Werewolf. Wolfman. Lycanthrope. Monster. But what I am to you is a saviour.' He pushed away from the stone and walked over. In a low voice, he said, 'Morven told me about your stepfather. I know what kind of man he is, I have seen his like before. They call me a beast, but he's the real monster.' He cocked his head again; it was a strangely canine gesture. 'And I can see you know that too. But if you let me in, little girl, I can solve two problems in one bite. You see, I need to eat human flesh every few years. It brings me new life, new energy, and stops me from being a wolf forever.

'So, I need something – or someone, and you need rid of something – or someone. Can you see the solution?'

Despite the hatred for her stepfather, Purdey was appalled. She backed away, pulling her cloak tight about her shoulders. 'That's monstrous. I won't let you in.'

He shrugged. 'That is your decision. But I shall be waiting not far off, in case you change your mind.' With that, he strode away. As Purdey hurried home, distant wolf howls echoed through the night; it brought her no comfort to think that they were just Branok.

~

Purdey had half-expected to open the door and find her stepfather sitting in the darkness, triumphant at having caught her out. But she entered the cottage and crawled into bed without discovery. After that, sleep was unbearably slow in coming.

The next morning, at the breakfast table, she could barely stifle her yawns. She tried to avoid looking at Isaac, who had woken up in a foul mood.

Ignorant of this fact, Tressa bounded up to her father and tugged on his arm. 'Papa, can we go to the fair today?'

'No. We went yesterday,' he said, not raising his eyes from his food.

Tressa pouted. 'But I want—'

'Enough!' roared Isaac, snatching his arm back with such force that Tressa was nearly knocked off balance. 'I said no, you little brat, and I mean it. Not today.'

'But it'll be gone tomorrow,' Tressa said in an

almost inaudible whisper. Isaac glared at her, and she quickly sat down.

An unpleasant silence descended over the breakfast table. From the corner of her eye, Purdey saw a tear roll down Tressa's nose. Her little sister might be the favourite child, but even she had taken the brunt of Isaac's foul moods before and feared his anger.

'Perhaps I could take her,' Margaret said in a soft, soothing voice, 'when I've finished around the house. After all, I haven't been either and we could—'

Isaac's hand whipped out so fast that Margaret didn't have time to flinch. The blow caught her across the cheek.

'What is it with you women?' he hissed. 'You conspire against me to empty my purse, make me a laughing stock. I won't have it. D'ya hear? I won't have it.' He rose and strode out of the house.

Margaret gave her daughters a small, tight smile. 'Your father didn't sleep well. We should all treat him with great respect and care today.'

'Yes, Ma,' Tressa said quietly, picking at her bread.

Purdey said nothing, but her mind whirled

with thoughts, and she couldn't stop glancing at the glowing red mark on her mother's face.

~

Isaac's black mood persisted for most of the day and only lightened after an unexpected visit from one of the knucklebone players from yesterday's fair. He and Isaac sat in the late afternoon sunshine, rolling dice, wagering coins, and since Isaac came off the better, he was all smiles when he came in for dinner.

His good mood put smiles on both Margaret and Tressa's faces, but Purdey kept hers perfectly neutral. She was trying to weigh everything in the balance. Despite their light-heartedness now, her mother and Tressa had been afraid and withdrawn for most of the day. And her mother kept touching the bruise on her face as if checking whether it had vanished yet.

When Isaac had struck her mother, anger had surged through Purdey; she'd felt both hot and cold at once. If Branok had come knocking at that moment, she would have gladly let him in. The dark day hadn't done much to lessen her resolve.

But now, as she sat amid her smiling family,

Purdey felt monstrous herself for considering such a brutal act. Isaac was laughing and joking, ruffling his daughter's hair, and smiling at his wife. Even his glances in Purdey's direction seemed to hold nothing except tenderness.

She looked at the smiles around her. *Can I really destroy this?*

This moment is but a small ray of happiness, a voice in her head told her, *it won't last.*

After dinner, the four of them sat before the fire again, doing the same as they had last night. The warmth of the fire was just lulling Purdey into a light doze when a howl split the silence. It sounded as if the beast was right outside the door.

Tressa screamed and scrambled onto her father's lap. 'A wolf! Papa, a wolf!'

'Hush now, I'll protect you,' he said, rubbing at her back.

'But it will get in and eat us,' Tressa wailed, trembling all over.

'It will not. We have good strong doors and shutters. If it *is* a wolf and not just Judson's old mutt got loose again,' Isaac added with a chuckle that sounded more than a little forced.

Tressa pointed at the fireplace. 'In the story, the wolf came down the chimney.'

Isaac stroked his daughter's hair soothingly. 'That's just a story. It wasn't real.'

I know it is a real wolf out there, Purdey thought, *and I know its name.*

They sat for a while longer until Margaret declared it time for bed. Without any repetition of the howl, Tressa had calmed and was half asleep on her father's lap. Margaret carried her into the room the two girls shared while Isaac checked the doors and windows.

Purdey undressed quickly and snuggled under the blankets next to her sister. Tressa had woken a little when placed into the cold bed, but now she curled up against her sister's warmth and fell back to sleep.

Purdey lay in the darkness, listening. She heard the wooden creak of someone turning over in bed next door. The hoot of an owl sounded outside, answered a moment later by another owl that was much closer. A soft howl rose through the night, and Tressa moaned in her sleep.

'Hush,' Purdey said, stroking her sister's hair.

The howl came again, and Tressa sat bolt upright in bed. 'What was that?' she squeaked, pulling the blankets up to her chin.

'Just a dog. Now, why don't...' Purdey fell silent as they heard a creature snuffling and scratching outside their window.

It's Branok, come to claim his meal.

Tressa slid to the edge of the bed. 'I'm going in with Ma and Papa,' she squeaked.

'No! Don't!' Purdey called, but Tressa was already halfway out of the door.

Please don't leave me.

She heard the creak of her sister climbing into Margaret and Isaac's bed, then low voices. There was a louder creak and then the slap of bare feet coming towards her room. Purdey pulled the blankets up to her chin.

Isaac appeared at the door, carrying a candle. He placed it on the table next to the wall.

'Tressa said she heard noises outside your window. Is that true?'

Purdey's heartbeat was so loud in her ears that she couldn't tell if the snuffling sounds were still there or not. 'Just a fox or something.'

Isaac walked to the window and stood silently, listening. Then he said, 'The others are curled up in our bed. You should come too, so I can keep all my girls safe.'

Purdey's mouth was so dry it might have

been coated with sand. 'No, thank you. I am safe here.'

Isaac regarded her for a long time, the shadows playing across his face as the candle flame flickered. 'Is that so?' He glanced at the door and licked his lips. 'Maybe I should stay a while to make sure you're not scared of the large, hungry wolf.'

He sat down on the bed and instantly Purdey was up, throwing the sheets off her and racing for the door. She felt his fingertips brush her arm as he tried to catch her. She headed straight for the front door. When she reached it, she unlocked it, but then her hand hovered over the latch.

'Come here, you little slut!' Isaac roared. She spun round to see him advancing on her. 'I saw those boys looking at you at the fair. I know what they were thinking.' His eyes narrowed. 'Is that why you wanted to be alone in there? Were *you* thinking about *them*?' She could see the fury blazing in his eyes. He was only a few steps from her now. 'Such filthy thoughts. I'll teach you what—

Purdey lifted the latch and tugged the door open. She'd rather be devoured by a beast with hair on the outside than be savaged by one who hid his fur on the inside. But before she could take a step outside, a large brown wolf cannoned past her.

Knocked off balance, Purdey cried out as she hit the floor. She had the briefest glimpse of her stepfather's shocked face before he vanished under a snarling mass of fur. His scream was short-lived, swiftly replaced by a wet gurgle and the sound of ripping flesh.

Pressing herself up against the door, Purdey couldn't do anything except watch with horrified fascination as the wolf went about its feast with speed and relish.

A white face appeared at one of the bedroom doors as Margaret looked out. Her hand flew to her mouth and then she stumbled back into the darkness. A moment later, her face was back at the gap, her eyes fixed on Purdey. Margaret's lips formed a single word: Run.

The wolf looked up from its meal, straight at Margaret who slammed the door shut with a whimper. Then it turned to Purdey. Blood coated its snout, and a string of gory saliva stretched down before breaking and dropping to the floor.

Looking into those blood-drunk yellow eyes, Purdey couldn't see any trace of the smiling man who let children bob for withered apples for a quarter-pence a turn. The beast's lip curled up, revealing sharp fangs with stringy meat caught between them. It began to advance on her.

'Branok,' Purdey said, her voice as sharp as a whip. The wolf shied away then shook its head as if trying to dislodge something inside its own skull. When its eyes found her again, they were a soft hazel, the eyes of a man. The wolf came forward and stood before her, its head cocked in such a familiar way.

'Thank you,' Purdey whispered, reaching out to stroke behind its ears; that seemed to be the only place that wasn't blood-splattered. 'I hope you enjoyed your meal.'

The wolf leaned forward, and for one awful moment, Purdey thought she'd been wrong and it was going to sink its fangs into her arm. But it merely licked her wrist, as a dog might. Its tongue left a bloody smear on her skin.

Suddenly, the creature tilted its head, its ears pointing forward. A low growl sounded from its chest before it bounded through the door. Purdey stood up and looked out into the night.

She saw the flash of brown fur darting away into the trees on her left, then her gaze was drawn to a glow approaching from the right, along the road from town. A group of men appeared carrying rusty swords, sharp axes, and various farm implements. The glow was coming from the flaming torches that they carried.

The man in the lead, whom Purdey vaguely recognised as a blacksmith, halted abruptly when he saw her standing in the doorway. The other men piled up behind and their murmuring conversation died away.

A voice from the crowd called out, 'That's Isaac Marrak's daughter.'

The blacksmith came towards her slowly and cautiously. 'Is Isaac Marrak your father?'

She held his gaze levelly. 'No. My father was Ross Teague. Isaac was my stepfather.'

The blacksmith raised an eyebrow. 'Was?'

Standing as she was in the doorway, Purdey had been blocking their view of what lay behind her. Now she stepped aside. The blacksmith turned away, his hand clamped to his mouth. The rest of the crowd tried to peer inside as well, many turning away just as the blacksmith had done.

Trengrouse the baker emerged from the crowd. Swallowing hard and being careful to look at Purdey and not into the house, he asked, 'Is the beast still inside?'

'No.'

'Which way did it go?'

Purdey resisted the urge to glance towards where she'd last seen Branok. Instead, she pointed a little to the right of the path they were on. 'It bounded out of the door just moments before you appeared. I saw it run along the gully there. It must have gone right past you.'

The crowd exploded into uproar.

'It's gone back to the town!'

'Our wives! Our children!'

'Kill it!'

As one, they surged back the way they had come. Purdey watched them go before shutting the door. Then she was faced with the lump of meat that had once been Isaac Marrak. Staring at his bloody remains, she felt a curious sense of sadness, but it was not for him; it was for her mother and sister who would truly miss him. For herself, she felt only relief.

She started towards her mother's bedroom then went back to where the cloaks hung. Taking down her beautiful red cloak, she laid it over the corpse.

Stepping back, she smiled with satisfaction. 'There,' she murmured. 'Now you won't scare the others, and the blood won't show through the red. Perhaps it was worth a whole silver penny after all.'

Outside, a wolf howled, and Purdey thought that the sound was filled with joy.

The Wild Hunt

'There,' smiled Sally, knocking the soot off her hands and leaning back on her haunches to admire her work. 'Doesn't the place look homelier with a nice roaring fire?' Her daughter smiled but looked unconvinced.

The holiday cottage was a little sparser than it had appeared in the advert, but Sally was still determined to make the best of it. After all, their own little place in the Scottish highlands, with no phone and no way for her ex-husband to contact them, was ideal. She wouldn't let Katy's Christmas be as bad as last year's.

'Go on, my little Ophelia,' said Sally, 'go and unpack – it'll look better with some of your mess around.'

Katy rolled her eyes. 'God, Mum. It was just the school play. You act like I was Ophelia at the Royal Shakespeare Company or something.'

'I can't help being proud,' Sally said with a grin. And she couldn't; it had been such a relief to see her normally withdrawn daughter launch herself into something so enthusiastically. It had really begun to feel as if they'd moved on from Andy.

As Katy trudged obediently upstairs, Sally stared out of the window at their surroundings. Rowan Cottage was high up on a Scottish hillside, separated from the rest of the village below by a vast expanse of open ground and a small local road. The closest house – still a five-minute walk away – belonged to the owner, a local farmer.

Being a converted barn, their cottage was all stone walls and pine beams, pleasant and airy but after being empty for a long time, it felt cold and damp. The windows on one side looked out over the village; the last afternoon rays of the winter sun shone through them, showing up a couple of smears that the cleaner had missed.

There was only one window on the other side of the house, in the kitchen, and it looked out onto the looming pine forest just yards beyond the end of the drive. The grass of the hillside stopped just a little way into the woods, as if afraid to venture in too far beneath the sharp needles and oppressive dark of the pines. No fence or hedge marked the end of the garden or the beginning of the forest, and it made Sally shiver every time she glanced that way while unpacking their food. She tried to shrug off the discomfort she felt as merely a consequence of two decades of city life. Yet there was something about the gloom between the tall, straight trunks that was distinctly sinister.

Upon Katy's reappearance, they wandered down to explore the village. The houses were sturdy, as befitted the harsh Scottish climate, but decorated with care. The front doors were made of thick wood, solid walls and fences made up definite boundaries, and looking beyond heavy curtains, Sally could see a fire blazing in every hearth.

Despite the fortress-feel of the houses, each dwelling was adorned with wreaths, evergreen sprigs, and garlands of holly and ivy. It looked festive and quaint if a little excessive.

They wandered into the local shop for some

essentials, and as she selected her purchases, Sally was aware of eyes and whispers following her.

They are not out to get you, she thought.

The counsellor's words came back to her: *You have value. Other people love you and respect you, even if he didn't. He told you they were out to get you as a means of control. They really aren't.*

This sentiment was confirmed when another shopper caught her gaze and smiled before saying, 'Merry Christmas.'

'And to you,' Sally replied.

'Got your holly wreath yet?'

'No. We've only just arrived. We're staying at Rowan Cottage.'

'Oh, you must get one. We all have one.'

'Thanks. Maybe.'

'No maybe about it. Christine!' the woman called to the shopkeeper.

'It's fine,' Sally said quickly.

'Got any wreaths left?'

'A couple,' Christine called back.

The woman smiled at Sally. 'There you go. It's all sorted.'

Sally could have hugged her daughter for coming up at that moment and asking if she could have a magazine, giving Sally an excuse to say, 'Excuse me,' and hurry off.

Christine was a rotund, friendly woman in a garish cardigan; she rang their purchases up on the till. 'You're up at Rowan Cottage, aren't you?' Her smile revealed lipstick smears on her teeth.

'That's right. My daughter and I are really looking forward to spending the season here. All those wreaths make it look so jolly and Christmassy.'

'And, of course, Gordon will have put one up on your door as well,' the woman said, a meaningful tone in her voice.

'Probably.'

'No, we don't have one,' Katy interjected.

There were mutterings from the next aisle along.

'Well, I'll just pop you some holly in, dear,' Christine said, bringing out a small wreath

'Oh, no, thank you,' said Sally. 'I wouldn't want to add anything to the house. It might upset Gordon if we went hanging up stuff like that.'

The whispers were replaced with a stony silence.

'I'm sure he won't mind,' Christine said carefully.

The woman from the aisle stepped forward. 'We all hang holly outside our doors. It's *tradition.*'

Someone at the back of the shop gave a small snort of derision, and another voice muttered, 'It's safe.'

Christine offered a warm smile in an apparent attempt to soften the icy atmosphere. 'I'll pop you some in anyway. No charge.'

Sally smiled politely, more eager to be away from this peculiarly uncomfortable atmosphere than to stick to her guns.

When they had left, Katy said, 'She was rather odd, wasn't she?'

'They're just not used to outsiders, I guess. After all, ours is the only holiday cottage for about ten miles.'

As soon as they got through the cottage door, Katy picked a book off the shelf and settled herself in front of the fire. Sally unpacked their extra groceries and dutifully went to hang the holly outside the door. There was a hole where a hook had clearly once been embedded in the wood. A brief search of the area revealed the hook lying a short way off in the grass. She pushed it back into the hole and hung up the wreath.

There. Now we're just like everyone else.

They had some lunch, and Sally was just settling herself before the fire with a cup of coffee when there was a knock at the door so unobtrusive it almost went unheard. Sally opened it and found a young man dressed in a thick duffel coat, cord trousers, and heavy boots. His cheeks were rosy with windburn, and his hair, which brushed the top of his tartan scarf, was sticking out at all angles.

'I'm Reverend McAllister. Call me Tom.'

She shook his hand. 'I'm Sally Hunter.'

'May I come in?'

Sally hesitated. He was a vicar, sure, but he was also a man, and a stranger at that. Andy would have hated her inviting a strange man in, and old habits died hard. But with his windblown, cheerful look, he seemed harmless. And quite cute, she had to admit. It had been a long time since a cute guy had wanted to talk to her.

'Sure,' she answered, stepping aside.

After pouring him a coffee, she took Tom into the sitting room, prompting Katy to look up and offer a friendly hello before returning to her book.

'I come with the pleasant duty of inviting you to the Gathering tonight,' said Tom taking a seat.

Katy looked up with sudden interest. 'That's an old local tradition,' she said eagerly. Tom looked at her in surprise, and she held up the book of local folklore she had been reading. 'It says in here that every year on the winter solstice, the Wild Hunt rides out. It's a host made up of the dead, the damned, and all manner of evil creatures. Anyone unlucky enough to fall in their path would meet with a horrible death or be forced to join the Hunt for eternity. Since their prey is human souls, the local villagers all used to congregate on sacred ground for safety, and this eventually turned into a regular celebration as the true meaning was lost in folklore.' She glanced at her mother. 'No wonder everyone in the shop was so insistent you took the holly if they're so fond of this tradition.'

Tom frowned. 'Gordon didn't leave you a wreath? But I saw one on the door.'

'Christine gave us that. I'm sure Gordon just forgot,' she added quickly, seeing Tom's frown deepen.

'No one ever forgets. It's tradition.'

There's that word again.

'Of course,' Tom hastily added, 'as a man of God I don't hold with pagan beliefs, but in this case there's no denying it brings out the festive cheer in everyone, so I don't raise too much of a fuss. So, will you be coming then?' There was an uncalled-for earnestness in his voice.

He's just being friendly. Stop overanalysing.

'We'd be delighted to,' said Sally, and Tom visibly relaxed. 'If outsiders are allowed, of course,' she added teasingly.

'Absolutely! All are welcome.' Sally liked the way his smile reached all the way to his eyes. She could feel a blush rising in her cheeks, and she caught a glimpse of Katy giving her a grinning thumbs-up.

'Thank you for coming, Reverend,' she said.

'It's Tom,' he reminded her.

Sally smiled shyly. 'Sally. Well, goodbye now. We shall see you tonight.'

Once the door was closed, Sally decided to stay in the kitchen, doing the washing up. Her plan was foiled by her daughter coming to stand in the doorway, still grinning.

'He was nice,' she said meaningfully.

Sally didn't raise her eyes from the washing up. 'He's a vicar. They have to be nice to everyone. Now—'

A monstrous knocking prevented her from finishing her sentence. Wiping the suds from her hands, Sally opened the door and found a far less pleasant man standing on the step. His skin was like cracked leather, and he slouched over a thick walking stick which had evidently been used to create the din.

He glared at her from under thick eyebrows, his strong jaw set in displeasure.

'What have you been doing, sticking holes in my door?'

'I'm sorry?' Sally said, somewhat confused.

The man gestured angrily at where the wreath had been hanging up. 'There. In the door. A hook.'

'There was already a hole,' Sally said defensively. 'I found the hook and I put it back.'

The man shook the holly wreath at her menacingly. 'I should have your deposit back for that.'

'Deposit? Oh, so you're Gordon Macleod. I'm so sorry. I didn't mean any harm. I'm Sally, this is my daughter,' she added, stepping aside so he could see Katy, who'd been peering around her. 'Katy, this is the gentleman,' she forced the word out, 'who owns Rowan Cottage.'

'Hello,' Katy said quietly and received a scowl for her trouble.

'I'll be taking this with me,' Gordon said, brandishing the wreath again. 'And just make sure you don't knock any more holes in my house, alright?'

He turned away without waiting for an answer, but Sally called after him anyway. 'Of course! Sorry. And Merry Christmas!'

She shut the door and Katy stared at it, puzzled. 'I thought those holly wreaths were a village tradition or something.'

'Who knows,' said Sally with a sigh, returning to the washing up. 'But I guess we'll just have to be the unconventional outsiders for this year.'

~

That afternoon, Katy insisted on a walk in the woods to blow away the cobwebs. Sally was reluctant – the darkness and total isolation which lurked beneath the branches made her feel nervous, but Katy was determined.

Walking into the gloom of the trees was like stepping into the grinning jaws of a carnivorous beast.

'The book said this is a corpse road,' Katy explained. 'The coffins would be carried along it from all the surrounding hamlets to the local church. This is supposed to be the course the Hunt would follow.' Katy was chattering happily away, but the anxiety Sally had felt ever since they stepped into the forest was steadily growing. It was so suffocating with the trees pressing in on all sides, and it was so quiet. No rustles, no birdsong. It was eerie.

Sally saw her daughter's eyes gleam in the gloom; Katy loved all things macabre and was thoroughly engrossed by her surroundings.

'And over here,' said Katy, pushing aside some of the overhanging branches, 'is the spot where the coffin carriers would rest. See – it's a circle surrounded by holly bushes and hawthorn, protection just in case the dead took a walk while they rested.'

'Charming,' said Sally nervously. A skittering noise behind her made her jump, her skin prickling. 'We'd better get back or there won't be time to get ready for the Gathering.' She was embarrassed by how relieved she felt when her daughter agreed.

But they'd only gone a few steps when Katy cried out, 'Oh, just a minute!' She raced back to the corpse stone and started tugging at the holly bush.

'What are you doing?' Sally called out, but she received no answer.

A few minutes later, Katy returned, beaming, and brandishing a couple of holly branches. 'Here. We can lean these up against the door. Grumpy Gordon whoever-he-was can't complain, and those women in the shop can't tell us off about their local tradition either.'

Sally beamed and hugged her daughter. 'I wish I was as resourceful as you.'

~

As they walked down into the village that evening, there was no doubt as to where all the inhabitants were: the houses stood dark and vacant while the church hall spilled forth light, music, and voices from every window. Holly, mistletoe, and Christmas roses bedecked the walls and the gravestones as well, which Sally thought was a peculiar touch. Inside, baubles and tinsel had been squeezed in wherever there was room, and a great fire burned in an enormous hearth at the far end. Sally hadn't ever seen a fireplace in a church hall before, and this one was particularly impressive with an ornately carved mantle made of dark wood and festooned with greenery.

Most of the villagers themselves were dressed in bright colours, but Sally's eyes were instantly drawn to those clothed in browns and black who wore an assortment of masks. There were devils, ghouls, hounds, skeletons, horses – all mingling with the throng, laughing and chattering away. It was somewhat surreal.

'Glad you could make it, Sally,' said Tom as he approached with three glasses of punch. He held one out to Katy who accepted it before politely excusing herself, throwing a look in her mother's direction.

'Have you met your landlord, by the way?' Tom asked, steering her in the direction of a sour-faced man that Sally recognised only too well. Gordon's eyes widened as they approached.

'Yes, I met Mr Macleod today,' Sally said with forced politeness. 'And again, I'm sorry about the door.'

'Don't mention it, no problem. Here, have a mince pie,' Gordon said, offering her a plate he was holding.

'No, thank you,' Sally said.

'Well, maybe your daughter would like one,' Gordon said, hastily walking away.

'What happened with the door?' Tom asked in a low voice.

'Oh, he didn't like the holly wreath I hung up. He said I'd put a hole in his door, which I hadn't, but I don't think he was very happy anyway.'

'But you still have the wreath on your door, don't you?' Tom's smile had dimmed dramatically.

'No, but don't worry,' Sally added quickly, 'Katy and I got some from the wood. Holly, I mean. It's not as pretty as everyone else but, well, we wanted to fit in. So we rested it against the doorstep.'

Tom's smile returned, although he looked a little shaken. 'Oh, well, that's alright then. Sorry, but tradition is very important to us, and I want you to feel a part of our community while you are here, at Christmas time.'

The blare of a hunting horn made them both jump. At this signal, the masked villagers ran howling and whooping through the crowd, chasing children and adults, eliciting squeals of delight from all.

'The Hunt has begun!' someone called out.

Sally laughed heartily at the look on Tom's face when a huge brute of a hell hound grabbed him from behind and whisked him away into the crowd.

The evening was better than anticipated; rather than being ignored as an outsider, everyone was friendly and eager to talk to her. Sally found the festivities infectious and she wasn't the only one; Gordon broke character and awkwardly offer Katy a mince pie which she accepted with a gracious smile. Every so often, the horn would sound and the Hunt would be on the rampage again.

Sally got so swept up in the revels that it was a full fifteen minutes before she realised she had lost sight of Katy. Having scanned the hall, Sally went into the abandoned kitchen to find Gordon standing in the corner, smoking a crumpled cigarette.

'If you're lookin' for the lass, she's gone home,' he offered with a sly smile. 'Said she felt sick, left five minutes ago. Bet you can catch her if you run.'

Sally picked up her coat, keeping one eye on Gordon. He was watching her with an intensity that she didn't care for.

'Please give Tom my apologies,' she said.

Gordon made a noise that could have been a yes or a no, but she didn't want to hang around and find out which.

Stepping out into the night was like nothing she had ever experienced. It was so icy that her fingers went numb within seconds, and she walked briskly to stave off the overwhelming cold. But she could see Katy just ahead, and she hurried to catch her up.

Back at the church, Gordon watched the two figures heading up the hill. With a chuckle, he called after them, 'You've forgotten yer holly!'

'Gordon?' asked a voice behind him.

The farmer spun round guiltily as the Reverend came to stand next to him. When Tom caught sight of the two receding figures, his expression turned to one of horror.

'You *know* that no one must leave until midnight.'

Gordon shrugged, unrepentant. 'Girl was sick. Couldn't stop them, could I?'

'You could have warned them,' Tom said, his shock turning to anger.

'They're outsiders. What do they matter?'

'Everyone matters,' Tom muttered, pushing past him and out into the night.

Gordon leaned out but didn't step over the threshold of the church. 'That's what *your* Lord teaches, vicar, but there's a different lord out tonight, and he has different rules.'

~

'I really would have been fine on my own, Mum,' Katy said with a hint of reproach.

'I know, honey, I just didn't like the idea of you being ill alone.'

Katy sighed. 'I feel much better now. Bit of fresh air. Must have been something I ate.' Katy glanced behind them then stopped with a frown. 'Isn't that Reverend McAllister running towards us?' she asked, pointing back at the village.

Sally turned and saw that Tom was indeed hurtling towards them. He didn't stop, just grabbed their hands and started pulling them onwards.

'Quick, we have to get to the cottage,' he said, gasping, 'we're too far away from the hall.'

'What's wrong?' Sally asked. When he didn't answer, she wrenched her hand out of his grip. Tom turned with frustration blazing on his face, but then his eyes flicked to something behind them and his face fell. Both Sally and Katy turned round.

Under the nearly full moon of the longest December night came raging the real Wild Hunt. Hounds of all shapes, sizes, and disfigurements bayed in anticipation, and behind them came the dead, the damned, and riders carrying torches which blazed blood-red and orange. Screams of pleasure mingled with those of pain as the tumbling mass forged its way through the village and up the hill towards them, the hounds speeding ahead. Even from this distance, the misshapen, bloated, and deformed bodies of the riders were appallingly evident. They moved with frightening speed, and Sally felt the breath catch in her throat.

'Is that—?'

'Yes,' Tom said grimly, 'and they're going to reach the house before us.'

'This way, come on!' Katy yelled, speeding off towards the wood. It curved around the hillside and, from where they were, it was much closer than their cottage.

Sally grabbed Tom's hand and dragged him, just as he'd pulled them. He resisted for a moment, apparently mesmerised by the sight, then he turned and ran with them.

Sally's heart was pounding in her chest, the cold air stinging her face. As she reached the edge of the forest, the baying of a hound, sounding impossibly close, made her turn. One hound was indeed outpacing the others and bearing down on them. For a moment, Sally was frozen in shock, then she stared around for something she could use to defend herself. But Tom came to her rescue first, swinging a hefty fallen branch in the face of the hound as it launched itself at her. With a pained squeal, it tumbled backwards, kicking up blood and snow.

The other hounds had caught up by now, and Sally felt sure that they must be done for. But the beasts fell on their downed brother, even as the hound struggled to its feet. Incensed by the smell of fresh blood, the creatures tore their brethren to bloody pieces. Sally ran headlong into the trees to escape its dying screams.

The dark of the forest was almost absolute.

The three of them held hands, struggling on together, lifting each other up when one of them stumbled.

But then an eerie red light lit up the trees as the Hunt surrounded and stalked its prey. Now the darkness was seething with black shapes that circled but didn't attack. Sally couldn't tell what they were waiting for, but she was grateful for any delay that might deliver them from this terrible fate.

Katy stifled a sob, and Sally hugged her daughter closer. Tom began to mutter a protective psalm under his breath, which earned them a chorus of snarls and obscenities from their pursuers.

'Look!' Katy pointed ahead, and Sally could have sobbed with relief at her wonderful daughter.

'Thank God,' Tom said, his voice choked.

Ahead of them was the resting stone of the corpse road, surrounded by holly and hawthorn. They picked up their pace, and the hounds around them became more agitated, running around and across their path, their howls now a frenzied yapping in their desperation to prevent their quarry reaching sanctuary. Yet still something held the beasts back, and the three of them managed to reach the safety of the circle.

Without warning, Sally's arm was yanked painfully backwards as a hound seized Tom's ankle in its jaw and tried to drag him out of the circle. Tom howled in pain as a dark gush of blood spilled from between the animal's teeth, and Sally found herself in a grim tug of war.

'Mind out!' yelled Katy behind them and a sizeable rock went flying over their heads. There was a hollow crack as it hit the hound's ribcage. The animal's eyes rolled as the blood seeping out of its mouth became its own. Its jaw slackened, and Tom wrenched his ankle free, pulling himself entirely into the safety of the circle.

Kneeling by him, Sally could instantly see that Tom was in trouble. He was shaking, sweating, gasping for breath, and the wound was already inflamed, as if filled with poison. Sally was doing her best to make his scarf into a tourniquet when she realised someone was approaching them.

'Good evening, mortals.'

With the scarf safely secured, Sally stood up and turned to face a man dressed in dark greens and inhumanly tall. His eyes were wholly black;

looking into them was like looking down into a deep, crumbling well. His skin was an unnatural white and wrapped tightly around his bones like wet silk. An unwavering yet natural smile was fixed on his lips. Sally briefly thought he might have been handsome once, but now he was emaciated.

She realised that the Hunt around them had grown silent, not even the sound of breathing, just their dead eyes watching her, glistening dully in the torchlight. Sally felt faint but she forced herself to be still.

'Who are you?' she demanded.

'He's the leader of the Hunt,' Tom whispered behind them.

'Your churchman is right,' the man said with a voice that was hoarse and scratchy.

'Gwynn ap Nudd,' whispered Katy. The name ran through the horde as a whisper, chilling Sally to her core.

Gwynn smiled. 'That name will do as well as any other.'

'What do you want?' Sally asked, her voice shaking only slightly.

'Quarry.'

The Hunt trumpeted and cheered in a

cacophony of agreement. The leader fixed his gaze on Tom. 'Your friend there will not last the night, but then more fool him for thinking his petty words to an impotent god would save him in my domain.'

'But the holly will protect us,' said Katy, coming to stand by her mother. Gwynn turned to her; Katy met his gaze with her jaw set and no hint of fear on her face. Sally felt a surge of pride. 'This circle has protected people from the dead for centuries, and it will protect us now.'

'You are, of course, correct,' he said, and a glint passed across his soulless eyes. 'We cannot cross the circle but...' He gave a slight nod, and his hounds instantly began digging at the base of the holly bushes, urged on by the caterwauls of the Hunt.

'These holly trees are almost as old as me,' said Gwynn idly. 'Their roots go deep and no doubt it will take some time to undermine your protection. But break it we will.'

Behind them, Tom moaned, and Katy went to him.

'Is this some kind of game to you?' spat Sally.

Gwynn stared at her then let forth a peal of

laughter. 'But of course! The Hunt is the greatest game of all.'

'The greatest?' Sally said derisively. 'It's cruel and pathetic. There's no skill in chasing down exhausted and terrified creatures.'

He cocked his head, those black eyes fixing on her thoughtfully. 'Is there another game you find worthier of your time?'

'A game of wits,' Katy said suddenly. 'A puzzle. That's surely a better test of someone's worth.' Sally glanced her, and Katy said in a low voice, 'That's how you win, in the fairy tales. Don't you remember?'

Gwynn rubbed his chin. 'Wits, yes. Very well. I shall set you a challenge this winter's night. If you can find a gift for me before midnight, one worthy of the Lord of the Dead, I will exchange it for your lives.'

'Your beasts will tear me to shreds the moment I step out of here,' Sally said.

'I can assure you they won't.' Sally folded her arms, unconvinced. His eyes narrowed. 'Isn't the word of a god enough for you?' His voice was low, menacing.

'Don't play his foul games,' said Tom, but his voice was weak and filled with pain.

Katy looked unnaturally pale. At that moment, she truly looked like the spirit of Ophelia, surrounded by darkness and madness. 'It's better than the alternative, Mum. What choice do we have?' She looked down at Tom then nervously at the dogs, who had paused in their digging but still remained alert, ready for a command. Tears trembled on Katy's lashes, but she scrubbed them away. 'I know you can do it, Mum. You can think of something.'

Sally remembered her daughter up on stage, a white gown flowing about her, crying, 'O, woe is me, to have seen what I have seen, see what I see!' Her daughter had only been feigning despair then, but now true misery and fear filled Katy's eyes.

She turned back to Gwynn. 'Done.'

The Lord of the Dead grinned and held his hand up. Immediately his hunters pulled back, clearing a path for her. Sally took a deep breath then stepped out of the circle. One of the hounds growled, low and menacing; for a heartbeat, she thought she'd been tricked. But Gwynn aimed a kick at it and the beast slunk away.

As she walked through them, the horde pawed at the ground, yowling and snapping at her, but they did not attack. She felt unutterably lost as she kept her gaze straight ahead, trying to ignore the fiends who pressed close on every side.

Her pace quickened until, by the time she reached the edge of the wood, she was running at full speed. On the frosty hillside, she stumbled to a stop. It was like another world filled with light and human habitation and sanity.

Glancing back at the trees, she could see the hounds among them, watching her silently. Shakily, she started towards the Christmas lights twinkling below her. The cold air was immensely welcome as a faintness had been creeping over her in the oppression of the forest. As she ran, her head began to clear.

She hammered on village doors as she passed them, calling out to those inside. But none of them opened and the windows remained dark.

Stupid, stupid! she cursed inwardly. *They're all at the church hall.*

She made her way there without delay, but dread coursed through her when she realised the lights were on but it was silent inside.

'Open up! I need your help.' The silence remained unbroken but for her shout. 'Damn it, open up! It's your sodding fault that I'm caught up in all this.' She took a step back, breathing hard. She had to control her temper if she didn't want to sound like a madwoman.

Even if I'm caught up in madness. A half-remembered line from her daughter's play drifted into her head. *With a look so piteous as if he had been loosed from hell. I probably look exactly like that. And who'd open their doors to a madwoman?*

After a deep breath, she called out in a reasonable voice. 'Even if you don't care about me and my daughter, what about Tom? He's up there and he's hurt. He needs your help too.' There were whispers on the other side of the door, and hope started to bloom inside her.

'Go away! You'll draw them to us!' shouted a hysterical voice from inside.

Sally ground her teeth then screamed at the top of her lungs. 'Go to hell, the lot of you!'

'You first, bitch!' came an answering cry.

Sally staggered away from the church, looking up at the wood on the hill. *What if he lied? What if his hounds have dug them out and my daughter's being slaughtered right now?* The idea brought a rush of nausea and she bent over, retching.

She slumped down, defeat weighing on her like chains. Filled with misery, she looked around at the graveyard, at all the headstones. *I'm surrounded by the dead and none of them can tell me what they want.*

A burst of hysterical laughter escaped from her lips, then she cried out, 'Why don't you tell me what you want?'

The hysteria left her, taking the last of her energy with it. *Katy would know the answer. She loves riddles and macabre stuff. She would know. I should have let her come.*

Her gaze drifted over the gravestones, the names, the dates, the words.

Edith Sanderson.

Frank Wilson.

Margery and Eric Larrington.

Resting.

Fell asleep.

In God's care.

Beloved by family.

Cherished by his friends.

In memoriam.

In loving memory.

She stopped, staring at this phrase, an idea forming.

Katy.

Ophelia.

Practising her lines over and over.

Mum, did you know that Columbine is a flower associated with deceived lovers? And fennel, that weird fluffy thing, that's for flattery. That's stupid. And rosemary...

Sally leaped to her feet and started running towards the cottage. By the time she reached the door, her side was consumed by the pain of a stitch, but she ignored it as best she could. She raced round the kitchen, pulling open cupboards and draws.

It's here. I know it's here. I bought it for the potatoes and the turkeys. God damn it! Where is—? And then she had it in her hand.

She raced back out of the door, intending to run all the way back to Gwynn, but the stitch stole her breath and the looming trees stole her courage. She slowed to a walk, but a fast one, tripping over far more tree roots than she should have done. Black shapes kept pace with her and red eyes watched her from the trees on either side.

It seemed to take far too long to get back to the resting stone, but eventually she saw the glow of flaming torches ahead. She ran the last bit, sheltering her gift from the wind as if it was a guttering candle. Her legs were burning now as well as shaking. When she finally reached the Hunt, she was panting, almost doubled over.

Gwynn raised an eyebrow. 'Perhaps it's just as well we changed the game. I can't see you being much use as prey.'

'Did you get something, Mum?' Katy asked, her face alive with hope. Around her, the hounds were still digging, and only a few holly trees remained standing against their onslaught. Tom lay in a stupor, his head on Katy's lap.

Sally straightened up and held Gwynn's gaze. With a trembling hand, she held up her offering. He reached out and took the sprig of rosemary. His skin brushed hers, and her nerves screamed at the pain of absolute cold, but Sally did not flinch.

'Rosemary,' she said, 'for remembrance.'

Gwynn held the sprig to his nose, breathed its scent deeply and became lost in thought. Sally was aware that his host had fallen silent. Every rider was staring at the tiny green plant that Gwynn held while the mounts stood motionless. Even the hounds had stopped digging, their noses questing the air for that sharp scent.

Coming out of his daze, Gwynn looked at her, his black orbs sparkling with a cold, cruel humour. 'What a gift,' he murmured. 'After all, what could the dead desire more than to be remembered? You have found a worthy answer to my puzzle.' He tucked the rosemary into the buckle at his belt.

'We will leave you now, as promised, but hurry to a place of safety. If we come across you again this night, there will be no challenge, only the Hunt.'

'The Hunt! The Hunt!' bellowed the creatures around him.

Gwynn swung himself up into the saddle of a great black horse. He gave a small nod to Sally before turning his mount's head and charging off through the trees. His host raced after him, vanishing into the forest.

Sally rushed to Tom's side. He was feverish, but his soft brown eyes met hers and he smiled.

'Ah, you're back,' he said with relief. He squinted around. 'Are they gone?'

'Yes, but we have to get inside. Can you walk?'

'I think so.'

Sally and Katy helped Tom to his feet, and the three of them staggered back through the wood.

When they finally broke out of the trees and saw Rowan Cottage ahead, Sally couldn't stop herself from speeding up, nearly causing all of them to fall.

As they hurried towards the cottage, Sally's gaze was drawn to the church – the only building lit up for miles.

They really were out to get me after all, she thought wryly.

Then she was forced to concentrate on trying to help Tom over the threshold to Rowan Cottage and safety.

Despite the exhaustion that had washed over her the moment she'd locked the door, Sally found some final shreds of strength to clean Tom's wound, smear some antiseptic cream on it, and bandage it up.

'Thank you. I think it's feeling a little better already,' he said. 'Tell me, what did you bring for the Lord of the Dead?'

Sally exchanged a look with her daughter.

'There's rosemary,' Katy said quietly, 'that's for remembrance. Pray, love, remember.' She smiled at her mother. 'Ophelia couldn't save herself, but she saved us instead.'

~

As the last stroke of midnight rang out through the village, signalling the end of the Hunt, the congregation in the hall gave a collective sigh of relief. Many of them looked accusingly at Gordon, who was sitting in a corner.

He sneered at them. 'What are you all looking at?

'How could you let that girl go? She was just a teenager,' Christine said in a furious whisper. 'You sent her and her mother to their deaths.' Murmurs of agreement ran around the room.

'The Hunt needs quarry,' he snapped back. 'They're strangers here. Better them than us.' The glares continued, although plenty of people looked guiltily away, and he knew they agreed with him.

He rose to his feet. 'You're an ungrateful bunch of bastards. I'm going home, with a clear conscience.'

Gordon strode out of the room, resentment thick around him. He slammed the door behind him as he left then took several deep breaths. The air was bitingly cold, and he could smell snow coming.

'Going to be a fine Christmas,' he murmured as he started towards home. Going through the church gate, he snatched up a sprig of holly from a garland and twirled it idly between his fingers as he walked.

He was on the outskirts of the village when a tall, dark shadow stepped out of the gloom in front of him. Gordon found himself staring up into the smile of death.

'It's a fine evening for a walk, Gordon,' Gwynn ap Nudd said.

Gordon swallowed nervously, gripping the holly tight between his fingers. The Hunt should be over; this demon shouldn't be here.

'That it is, sir,' he replied. 'I trust you had good sport this evening.'

Gwynn shrugged. 'Not as good as you promised, Gordon. I set the woman a challenge and she passed with spirit. There was no chase at all.'

Gordon cursed under his breath. He could see other shadows now, forming out of doorways, crawling over roofs. He glanced over his shoulder, but he was too far from the sacred ground of the church now to make a dash for it.

'It's nothin' to do with me if you choose to let them escape,' he replied and saw Gwynn's eyes flash with a dark fire. He took a step backwards.

'I held up my end of the bargain.' Gwynn took a step forwards. Gordon took another two steps back.

'Besides,' he added, nervously waving the holly at Gwynn, 'there's nothing' you can do to me. I got me holly and it's past midnight. You got no power here no more.'

'The Hunt isn't over until our bargain is fulfilled. At least one soul, you said, for us to hunt and devour.'

'But... it's p-past midnight,' Gordon said, his teeth chattering with the intense cold that surrounded him, 'and I've g-got my h-holly.'

Gwynn smiled and it was an awful sight to behold. He gestured at the twig with distaste. 'You think this paltry token has any hold over me? A bargain with the dead is absolute and must be honoured.'

'But my holly—'

A flash of dark fur lunged towards him, and Gordon saw his whole hand being encompassed by the jaws of a huge hound. It took only a moment before the hound was gone again, and so was his hand. Gordon stared at the cauterised stump; it took a second for the pain to register through his utter shock, but when it did, Gordon screamed and fell to his knees. Yet even above the screaming, he could hear the sound of the beast crunching on his severed hand. Then the hound whined, spitting out the holly leaves before worrying at its gums where the sacred plant had pricked it all over.

Whimpering, Gordon looked up at the unsmiling face of the Lord of the Dead.

'You should be more careful with the deals you make,' Gwynn said, 'you promised me quarry, and I have come to claim it.' Gordon turned and started to crawl away, clutching his raw stump. 'But I like all my quarry to have a sporting chance,' Gwynn called after him, 'so I'll give you to the count of a hundred. One. Two. Three...'

Teeth in the
Shadows

It was the greatest feast Chiara had ever seen, but her stomach cramped so much she couldn't eat a bite. She glanced up at the high table where King Alessandro sat, Giada at his side. Chiara had known the woman since they were children; Giada had been a plump, healthy, and happy child, but sitting next to the king, she looked sick, and no wonder. Very few of those women who were put forward to become the king's second wife left the castle alive or whole.

Although Chiara could not hear their conversation, she could tell it was not going well. Giada had a slight stammer when she was nervous, and Alessandro was drumming his fingers on the table.

'That could be you up there,' her father, Edoard, whispered.

Chiara shuddered. 'I'm glad it's not.'

'You'd win his heart without a doubt,' Edoard said before ripping into a chicken leg.

Chiara's eyes strayed to the velvet cushion next to the king's goblet. She could just see the small mound of pink that was the late queen's hand, lying on the top. It was said that Alessandro never let it out of his sight, and even slept with it next to its pillow. Everyone in the hall had regularly seen him talk to the severed limb.

Alessandro smacked his hand down on the table and Giada flinched. The king glared at her then addressed the assembly. 'The feast is over.'

Snatching up his most treasured possession, Alessandro swept regally from the room. Immediately, servants converged on the tables to take the food away. If the king declared that dinner was over, then no one else was permitted to eat in the Great Hall. However, there was no law about taking food out of the hall and eating it in your private apartments. In the wake of the king's moods after his beloved wife's death, many of the nobles had learned to exploit this loophole to avoid an empty belly.

'Quick, Chiara, grab me that jelly,' Edoard urged.

Chiara swept the little pot of raspberry jelly from the table just as a servant was reaching for it. Her father added it to the other items he'd plundered.

Leaning across the table, he addressed an excessively fat man three seats down. 'Domenico, will you eat with me in my solar?'

'But of course,' Domenico replied with a broad smile. He glanced left and right then whispered loudly, 'I have a whole chicken beneath my jerkin.'

'Good man!' said Edoard with a chuckle. Then he sighed. 'I remember times when the king's great feasts carried on well into the night.'

'Was that when the queen was alive?' Chiara asked.

'No,' replied Domenico darkly, 'it was before she ever came here.'

~

With the feast abruptly ended, Chiara was filled with a nervous energy that left her pacing her rooms. Giada might have walked away from the high table alive (something which not all suitors achieved), but accidents had been known to happen to such women afterwards.

But Chiara's fear had ebbed for the moment, and that led to her stomach rumbling. Eating with her father was out of the question. Baron Edoard Girardi was very clear on where women should be when men dined – as far away as possible.

Summoning her maid, Chiara declared, 'I'm hungry, Luisa, and I can't sit still. Let's go into the town, find ourselves a warm taverna and some good food.'

'Yes, milady,' Luisa said with a deep curtsey and a mischievous grin.

Her father also held strong views about whether noble women should be allowed to go into town accompanied only by a maid, but since Chiara had slipped out three times already, she'd decided that this particular edict was as ridiculous as the rest.

Changing out of her court gown into a dark green rough spun overdress with a faded linen underdress, Chiara pulled on a heavy brown cloak to complete the transformation.

'Just like a taverna wench,' Luisa pronounced.

Luisa led them through hidden passages which the servants used to avoid cluttering up the fine corridors. With so many candles and oil lamps in the palace giving the air a hot and heavy texture, Chiara found stepping out into the cool night a blessed relief.

'Where to tonight?' Chiara asked as they hurried through the dark streets.

'The Queen's Jewels.'

Chiara frowned. 'Last night was The Queen's Rest and before that The Fine Francesca. Are all the tavernae named after the former queen?'

'Yes. King's orders.'

The Queen's Jewels was a good choice. It was brightly lit with sweet rushes on the floor and patrons who appeared friendly and good-humoured. The women ordered some spiced wine then took a corner table. Just as they were taking the first sips of their drinks, the door opened and a man in palace livery came in.

'Is it over then, Roberto?' the barman called out.

'It is, Stefan,' said the man, wiping his forehead, 'and I'm thankful for it.'

'Did this one survive?'

'Yes.' Some of the patrons put a fist to their hearts, an acknowledgement of divine blessing. 'For now, anyway,' the man added darkly.

Chiara felt a shudder run through her.

'Let's hope her father isn't fool enough to send her up again,' one man said.

Another snorted into his tankard. 'You'd be quicker looking for a purple duck among chickens than you would be looking for a sensible baron.'

'And their daughters are all empty-headed things,' the barman's wife added sagely.

'Is that so?' Chiara said before she could stop herself. All eyes turned to her, and she regretted speaking out. Softening her tone, she asked, 'You don't think they are victims of their upbringing?'

'Yes, it's so terrible to be born into wealth,' sneered Roberto.

'It is if you're forced to forfeit your life simply because you said the wrong thing at dinner,' Chiara said coldly.

'And what would you know about it?' asked the barman's wife sourly.

'As Baron Girardi's daughter, quite a lot.'

The whole company stared at her. Stefan shook his head. 'You're no baron's daughter, lass.' But his wife was frowning.

Roberto pointed at Luisa. 'I seen that one coming and going at the palace.'

'And the woman does have the bearing of a Girardi,' the barman's wife said.

'Sara's right. Look at her curly hair,' someone whispered. 'Just like the baron's.'

Sara drew herself up. 'Apologies, my lady. I spoke out of turn. Stefan, get her ladyship another glass of wine on our own coin.'

'Thank you,' Chiara said as the glass was placed before her, 'and I'll have some of that pottage, please. Using my own coin, of course.'

'You won't be used to our kind of rough eating,' Sara said as she brought them two bowls.

'I cannot eat a thing at court for fear. So, pottage in good company with merry faces and no hint of death is more welcome than even the choicest salmon or the lightest syllabub.'

As Chiara ate, she heard whispers running around the room. 'She's not as stuck up as the rest of them.'

'Quite pretty too, for an inbred noble.'

'What's syllabub?'

'Your father hasn't put you up to be the king's new bride then?' Stefan asked.

'No.'

'Still, you want to be careful on your way back to the palace, milady,' Sara said. 'There's terrible things hiding in the dark. You wouldn't want to come under the familiar's curse.'

'The what?'

Sara lowered her voice. 'Queen Francesca was a witch.'

'That's just a tale,' scoffed her husband.

Sara put her hands on her hips. 'Then why does the king still carry round her dead hand?'

'You cannot blame a dead wife for what a grieving man may do to ease his suffering,' Stefan declared.

'Can you blame her for murdering his sister?' Sara snapped.

'Princess Benedette died in an accident,' Chiara said. There was an uneasy atmosphere to the room now. 'She was out riding, her horse threw her, and her gown dragged her down into the depths.'

The silence stretched on so long she thought no one was going to reply. Then a man offered up, 'Some say her horse was bewitched and dragged her into the lake itself.'

'You ever been to Lake Ortino, milady?' Roberto asked. 'It's shallow for quite a way in. That horse must have thrown her really far if she landed in water deep enough to drown in.'

'And what about that girl last month who offered herself as the king's bride?' Sara mused. 'Livinia, I think. She fell down some stairs.'

'An accident,' Stefan said.

Roberto shook his head. 'One of the groomsmen from Baron Fontana's household said that they found scratch marks on her face, deep ones, made by claws, and on her hands too.'

'So, you'd better watch yourself, milady,' Sara said.

'This is just servant's gossip,' Chiara replied, even as she felt unnerved by how closely their words matched her own fears.

Sara bridled at that. 'Would you believe it from the mouth of the king's own sister?' she demanded.

'How can you ask a dead woman anything?'

'There is a way, for those that have the stomach. Outside the town, about two hundred strides along the road, there's a path that leads off into the hills. There's a bell there, a bell they'd ring to summon the coffin cart when someone had died in the far villages. The city gravediggers would meet the cart there and check the dead for infection before bringing them in to be blessed.

'It's different these days, with temples in

villages beyond the town where the dead can be shriven, but the bell is still there.'

'It's true,' another patron said. 'Back in the days of the War Kings, one of their number fell sick after a battle. No one could cure him, but a hermit rang the bell at half moon and summoned the dead. He found the king's greatest enemy had cut the king with a poisoned spear before he was killed. The dead gave the hermit the cure for it, and the king was saved.'

Sara leaned over the table, her voice low. 'So, if you want to know the truth of what's happening to your kind, milady, and you don't believe honest tavern folk, best go ask the princess.'

Chiara was prevented from replying as the door crashed open and another man in palace livery came in. 'Roberto, you have to come back.'

'What's wrong?' Roberto asked, paling.

'That poor lass tonight. She's taken to her bed, sobbing and raving about the shadows moving. Teeth in the shadows, that's what she keeps saying. There's a lot of commotion in the palace and we need more men.'

Roberto drained his tankard and hurried out. Chiara stared down into her goblet, conscious that all eyes in the taverna were now resting on her.

~

'Where are you going, milady?' Luisa called out as Chiara left the taverna and turned towards the city walls.

'To find that bell.'

Luisa caught her arm. 'You can't! It's not right, to summon the dead.'

'Didn't you hear him? Shadows with teeth. What if I can help Giada?' She lowered her voice. 'What if I need to help myself one day?' A visible shudder ran through Luisa. 'Go back to the palace. I'll find my way.'

The guards on the gate halted her, frowning at her drab garb, but when she showed them her family's signet ring, they stepped aside quickly enough.

Chiara had never thought of the town as noisy, but as she ventured into the deserted countryside beyond, she realised there were dozens of little sounds that were suddenly absent: the drip of an overflowing drain; the sound of doors opening and closing; distant footsteps, and the murmur of beggars as they asked for charity.

What surrounded her now was only

emptiness. The slap of her shoes on the road was the loudest noise around.

The moon was high and bright, although when it occasionally hid behind a cloud, she regretted not bringing a lantern. Nevertheless, she found the path she sought easily enough. By the time she reached the bell, Chiara was breathing hard from the steep climb.

The bell was situated in the dip between two hills, just by the side of the uneven path. A wooden cover protected the bell from rain, and although the leather bell-pull was showing signs of rot, it looked as if it would serve its purpose.

A large flat stone had been placed next to the bell, presumably for the coffin to rest on as its bearers waited for the coffin cart. Chiara sat down on it gratefully. The night was still and peaceful; it was hard to imagine that one of her oldest friends might, at this very moment, be writhing and screaming, caught in the middle of a waking nightmare. Warmth seemed to seep from her body at this thought, and she stood up hastily.

Gripping the leather cord tightly, Chiara rang the bell. She waited, listening.

Perhaps once isn't enough.

She sounded it again, then a third time. That final chime left an unpleasant ringing in her ears, and the air became heavy, difficult to breathe.

An instinct made Chiara step off the path and back onto the verge. Instantly, the ringing in her ears ceased and she could breathe easily once more. Curiously, she reached towards the path. As her fingers touched the air directly above it, she saw bright blue sparks dance over her fingernails, and she snatched her hand back.

Movement caught her eye, and she turned to see a host of white figures coming around the bend. They appeared to be made of light and cast an eerie glow on the path, although the illumination did not cross the verge and spill onto the grass.

The figures drew level with Chiara, and she looked at each of them carefully. There seemed to be no common link between them: old and young were there, men and women, some who walked erect, a sublime look on their face that gave them the appearance of heavenly beings, and others who walked as if still crippled with the pains that had plagued them in life.

As Chiara's gaze fell on one figure, her heart

gave a lurch. The woman's ghostly clothes were noticeably grander than those of the other phantoms, but what made her stand out was how her hair was plastered to her head and water dripped from her clothes.

Taking a deep breath, Chiara called out, 'Princess Benedette?'

The ghost paused and turned to her, the other phantoms flowing around her like a stream around a rock. Chiara could see the resemblance to Alessandro immediately. She moved forward to the edge of the path. 'Princess Benedette. Can I speak with you?'

'You may,' the woman said, drifting over. The ghost shone as brightly as if she were made of a thousand candle flames, but no heat emanated from her.

'It's about your brother. I need your help.' The ghost remained silent. More urgently, Chiara asked, 'Can you help me?'

'I don't know.'

This answer jogged a memory from tales Chiara had heard in the nursery. The dead could only answer direct questions. They could not speak their own minds, only respond to what was put to them.

'Can you tell me about Queen Francesca?'

'Yes.'

'Was she a witch?'

'Yes.'

'Did she kill you?'

'Yes.'

'How?'

'My horse ran into the water. I couldn't move. I drowned.' The ghost's tone remained steady and dull, as if she wasn't speaking about her own demise.

'Is there still a spell over the king?'

'Yes.'

'What spell?'

'I do not know.' Benedette's gaze had been somewhat unfocussed before, but now she looked hard at Chiara.

There is a question she wants me to ask, Chiara realised. *But what? She doesn't know what the spell was – how else can she help?*

Unless you don't need to know what a spell is if all you seek is to undo it.

'Do you know a way to break the spell?'

A flicker of relief passed over the ghost's features. 'Yes.'

'How?'

'The queen's hand has a ring. The white gem holds the enchantment. Remove it and the enchantment is undone. But...' Benedette's face twisted in anguish. 'Cannot... Only questions...'

'Is there something more you want to tell me?' Chiara said.

'Yes.'

'What is it?'

Benedette's wide eyes bulged. 'Familiar... beware... teeth in the shadows... the light will—'

Her words were cut off by the single sharp chime of the bell. The ghostly procession vanished.

Startled, Chiara turned and saw a creature had wrapped itself around the bell-pull. It had a long serpentine body, six stubby legs, each one tipped with ragged claws, and a rat-like tail; its head was that of an emaciated monkey. Its jaws opened, revealing needle-sharp teeth, and it gave a piercing shriek.

Chiara stepped backwards as the creature leaped for her. But as it emerged into the moonlight, it gave a squeal of pain. It darted back into the shadows where it hissed at her.

Benedette's words rose up in her mind, the

same that Giada had spoken in her ravings: teeth in the shadows.

It can't come into the light. It has to stay in the darkness.

Looking upwards, Chiara saw that although the half-moon was bright, there were several clouds in the sky that might obscure it at any moment.

With a last glance at the demonic little creature watching her with luminous eyes, Chiara raced down the path, heading back towards town. She was almost back to the road when a cloud slid in front of the moon. Behind her, a screech echoed around the hills.

The temptation to look over her shoulder was immense, but the road was uneven. It would do her no good to glance back only to stumble and fall. She did allow herself to look up and, with relief, saw that the obscuring cloud was almost completely past the moon. A moment later, the land was flooded with light again. Panting, she turned and watched the illumination spread out behind her, and she caught sight of a small creature darting into some trees.

There had to be several hundred feet between the road and the treeline, but the familiar had been fast; it could swiftly cross that distance the next time the moon was hidden. She turned and ran as fast as her aching legs would allow.

A sharp pain was developing in her side and her throat was raw with the cold night air. Another cloud was heading towards the moon, but the town gates were in sight now.

If I'm quick... She willed herself to go faster. The guards at the gate were staring at her, their spears held ready but uncertainty flickering on their faces.

The cloud slid across the moon when she was just ten strides from the gates. An animalistic screech heralded her attacker breaking cover. Moments later, a sharp pain ripped through her shoulder as the familiar landed on her back, its talons digging into her cloak. She screamed and twisted, trying to pull it off and getting her fingers bitten in the process. 'Get it off! Get it off!'

'Dear gods, what is it?' cried one of the guards.

The other guard lunged for the beast. He wore thick leather gloves reinforced with some kind of metal plate. He gripped the familiar by the neck and hauled it off Chiara. The creature swivelled round and bit down, then howled with pain, and the guard dropped it in surprise. The demonic creature pawed at its simian mouth before bounding away into the shadow of the walls, just as the moon emerged once more.

'What in all the heavens was that?' the other guard asked.

The man who'd been bitten shook his head. 'I don't know, but it was fey whatever it was. Did you see how it was when it bit me? Couldn't stand the taste of the iron on my gloves. Come inside, quickly, milady,' he added.

Chiara was only too happy to oblige.

~

Chiara couldn't remember the way through the servants' passages, so she was forced to walk through the main part of the palace. She kept her hood up and her head down. Although a couple of nobles sneered at her, no one challenged her.

Throwing open the door to her rooms, she found Luisa pacing backwards and forwards. Her expression of relief swiftly changed to one of shock when she saw just how bad her mistress looked.

As Luisa helped her with her cloak, brushed

out her tangled hair, and wiped the mud from her face, Chiara related all that had occurred. When she finished, Luisa was pale. 'Let's see this injury then, milady.'

Wincing at the pain, Chiara pulled down the shoulder of her dress. 'How bad is it?'

'They're some nasty puncture wounds, but hot water and brandy will do them wonders.' Luisa fetched the necessary materials; Chiara gritted her teeth against the intense stinging as her maid cleaned the wounds. She tried not to think about what filth might have been on that creature's claws, now buried in her flesh.

When Luisa was finished, she wiped her forehead and said, 'Gods preserve us, but I need a drink milady. Shall I bring us both some hot wine?'

'No. It'll only send me to sleep,' Chiara said, curling up on the bed.

'Sleep might be best for you, after everything.'

'No,' Chiara said sharply. 'I must stay awake, and in the light. Bring in more candles.'

'It won't get in here, milady,' said Luisa soothingly. Chiara glared until her maid hurried to comply.

Just keep me alive until morning, please gods, Chiara prayed, *and grant me some way to break this witch's curse and be free of her demon.*

Luisa's fussing and fidgeting became too much for Chiara, who sent her away before curling up at the corner of her bed, next to the lights. Despite her uncomfortable position, Chiara's exhaustion was overwhelming, and she soon slipped into sleep. Her dreams took her to a cliff edge, looking down at the crashing surf. A wind whipped around her, smelling more of smoke than salt.

Chiara jolted awake, realising she really could smell smoke. The room was gloomy, almost dark, and she instantly saw the reason why. The window was open and the breeze was extinguishing the candles one by one.

Scrambling off the bed, Chiara dashed to the window and slammed it shut just as the last candelabrum was guttering. There was a thud as something threw itself against the glass, and Chiara saw two gleaming yellow eyes looking in at her.

The door to her rooms opened. Chiara felt a rush of relief to see Luisa, but then she saw that her maid's eyes were glazed and she was carrying a pitcher of water towards the hearth. With horror, Chiara realised she intended to douse the fire.

'No!' Chiara lunged forward and seized the pitcher, trying to wrench it from Luisa's grasp, but her maid hung on grimly. As Chiara lost the tug of war, her eyes alighted on the poker. She thought of the guard at the gate. Would this be made of iron too?

Just as Luisa was drawing back to throw the water on the fire, Chiara seized the poker and swiftly pressed it to her arm. Luisa's eyes widened, and she dropped the pitcher to the floor. Then Luisa bent double and vomited up a pool of dark red slime.

She straightened, wiping the last of the foul stuff from her chin with shaking hands. 'I thought that wine tasted off.'

'I think you were enchanted and sent to douse the fire.' They both glanced at the window where two baleful eyes stared back at them for a moment before vanishing.

Chiara realised she was shivering. 'I think I will take some hot wine now.'

Luisa shook her head 'No more wine, milady. I'll get us some cider. Put the poker in the fire and we'll heat it up.' A sharp, hysterical laugh burst from her mouth almost as explosively as the slime had done. 'I'm most grateful that it wasn't in the fire before you pressed it to my flesh.'

Chiara hugged her tight. 'If it had been, I'd have let the fire go out rather than hurt you. Now, go get the cider.'

~

When day finally dawned, Chiara's eyes felt sore and gritty. Her back ached from sitting up all night, and her stomach churned from too much cider and terror.

'Do you think it is safe to sleep now?' Luisa asked as Chiara lay down.

'If that creature is to kill me by daylight, then so be it. I can't stay awake any longer. Tell my father I'm ill.' Luisa scurried out, and Chiara fell into a fitful sleep where small things with sharp teeth chased her through a great hall of stone pillars.

Luisa roused her just after midday. 'Why didn't you let me sleep?' Chiara asked groggily. The wound in her shoulder was throbbing.

'I thought it might be an enchanted sleep,'

Luisa said sheepishly. 'And I wanted to check on your wound.'

After Luisa had declared the wound red but uninfected, Chiara ate a little bread and cheese and drank some small ale. Then she went to the window, and in the glare of the bright sun, thought about what she was going to do.

Luisa returned as the sun was going down. Chiara washed and dressed hurriedly, wanting to be ready when night fell. But even though the two of them sat in her room, pokers held grimly on their laps, the familiar did not make a reappearance.

Eventually, the eighteenth bell of the day sounded and Chiara got unsteadily to her feet. 'That is the supper bell. I must go down and sit with the king.'

Luisa was aghast. 'Milady! Why would you do such a thing?'

'I have been thinking on it every moment I've been in this room, Luisa, and I have an idea on how to break the enchantment.' She looked at her maid levelly. 'If I can break the queen's spell, then I suspect that little creature will have no further power over us. Do you want to spend every night huddled near the fire, terrified that the lights will be put out and talons will reach for you in the darkness?'

Luisa shuddered. 'No, milady.'

'Then I must go and dine with the king.'

'Then at least let me put some rouge on your cheeks, milady. You look fairly ill, and the king'll not want to sit with someone so wan and exhausted.'

When Chiara entered the feasting hall, she felt a small knot of tension inside her loosen slightly. The king was at his table, and no one sat beside him. She had been worried that one of the other barons might have pushed his daughter on him tonight, but her way was clear. Clenching her trembling hands into fists, she walked the length of the hall. Those already seated must have sensed her intention as a gradual hush fell around her.

As she approached the high table, the king looked up in surprise. Chiara made a deep curtsey. 'I wondered if I might be permitted to dine with you and your good lady wife tonight, your majesty?'

A beaming smiled brightened the king's face and he suddenly looked like a young man again. 'We'd be delighted, wouldn't we, Francesca?'

Although he got no reply from the hand, his smile didn't shift.

The hall was blanketed in utter silence as Chiara climbed up onto the dais. 'My king,' she said, inclining her head to Alessandro, 'my queen,' she added, doing the same to the hand.

'How pleasant to have such agreeable company with us. Tell me, my dear, your name and where you come from.'

And with that invitation, Chiara's torment began.

The foul familiar chasing Chiara through the night had been intensely terrifying, but conversation with the king brought with it a different kind of fear. She was playing a dangerous game. At any moment, the king could turn round and accuse her of playing him for a fool. After all, she was holding a conversation where a severed hand was a silent third party.

The king spoke mostly to Chiara, turning to the hand occasionally to say, 'Isn't that so, dear?' or 'You would agree, wouldn't you, Francesca?' Generally, the king's phrasing suggested the answer he expected; but in one instance, as he spoke about the possibility of a war with a neighbouring nation, Alessandro said to his wife, 'But what are your thoughts, my dear?' A moment of silence followed where the king nodded, as if listening to a voice only he could hear. Then he turned to Chiara. 'My wife makes a valid point, but what do you think?'

Chiara found her tongue stuck to the roof of her mouth. How should she respond? One way she risked offence by saying something unpolitical; another way she might accidentally disagree with whatever he thought the queen had said. She had to choose her words carefully to avoid death or humiliation.

She gave a smile and hoped her voice didn't shake as she answered, 'The queen does indeed speak wisely, but we are only women, your majesty. I'm sure your wife would agree that we should bow to your greater wisdom as a man.'

The king clapped his hands together in delight. 'Why, what a charming girl you are, and so sensible. Baron Girardi!' he called across the room. 'Your daughter is the most sensible chit I've spoken to all season.'

Edoard got to his feet, his face as pale as the moon. He gave a slight bow. 'Your majesty is too kind to say so.' Before he sat down, he threw a pleading glance at Chiara, though what he was beseeching her to do, she could not tell.

Despite her dull terror, Chiara found herself fascinated by the detached limb. The queen had been dead two years, so the flesh should have rotted away by now. Yet the hand was pink and healthy, the skin smooth and unblemished.

For the last month, the king had ended his feasts early by storming out or stalking sullenly away. But tonight, he was in high spirits, and he kept everyone in the hall three times as long as he had the night before. Chiara was beginning to think that an end to her torment would never come when the king stood and gave her a deep bow.

'This has been the most pleasant evening I have enjoyed for some time, but I'm afraid matters of state must take my attention away from my guests.'

Chiara stood, trembling slightly. The moment was here; everything she had planned would either stand or fall in this one moment. 'It has been my honour, your majesty. May I ask if your wife could stay with me while you attend to such matters?'

Hardly daring to breathe, Chiara watched

Alessandro's face crease into a frown. He looked down at the severed hand.

'No,' he said slowly, 'I think not. You will forgive me, but I cannot bear to be parted from her.'

Chiara cursed silently, but there was still one chance left.

'Quite understandable,' said Chiara, her mouth dry. 'Then let me show my loyalty to you both and my thanks for such a splendid evening.' Daringly, she reached out and took the king's hand in her own, bending forward to kiss his fingers. She feared Alessandro might be outraged at this boldness in touching him, but the king merely smiled.

'A young girl who knows the traditions of fealty. Your father has raised you well.'

'May I pay the same courtesy to your wife?'

'But of course.' He lifted the velvet cushion and held it out towards her. Chiara's stomach roiled as she lowered her face towards the hand. This close, she could see that the flesh where it had been severed from the queen's arm was still wet and stringy, as if it had been sliced off only a few minutes ago.

She reached out and picked up the hand. Her

mind told her that it was supple and warm while her fingers told her that the flesh was hard and cold. Waves of revulsion washed through her as she brought that dead thing to her face. Before she pressed her lips to the fingers, a sweet, cloying scent filled her nose, and she had to fight down a surge of bile.

Closing her eyes, she kissed the hand, her lips telling her mind that the thing was icy cold.

Even though she wanted to fling such foulness from her, she replaced the limb slowly on the cushion. As she drew her own fingers away, she gripped the enchanted ring and slipped it off the finger.

The king's eyes instantly unfocussed, and his skin took on a pale, waxy sheen. Staggering a little, he reached out to steady himself on the throne.

On its little velvet cushion, the hand started to decay in an extraordinary manner. The skin stretched then split, the flesh fell from the bones, becoming dust before it hit the velvet. Even the bones cracked and crumbled to a coarse white powder.

'What happened?' Alessandro asked in a hoarse whisper. Both he and Chiara looked down at the ring she held in her hand. The clear crystal on it winked in the firelight, and Chiara had the sudden overwhelming urge to slip it onto her own finger.

He would adore me then. I could be queen. I could advise him, we could rule wisely, I could—

With a cry of disgust, Chiara dropped the ring on the floor. Then she picked up the chair she had been sitting on and slammed the leg down onto the crystal which shattered into a million sparkling fragments.

~

When Chiara and her father finally left the palace after a month of being the king's honoured guests, Alessandro would hear of nothing less than that they should have his own litter bearers and royal box to travel home in.

Edouard actually blushed and tried to refuse this honour, but Alessandro insisted. After the first seven miles of the journey had passed, Edouard was forced to admit that it was a far more comfortable way to travel than riding a horse. It was so comfortable, in fact, that he fell asleep for the rest of the journey.

Chiara watched the landscape beyond the

box's windows and felt at peace. The realm would change now, the court would be better run, and all in the land would benefit.

As the sun started to sink, she reached out to pull the curtain across. A clawed hand appeared on the sill, a withered simian head following it. With a cry, Chiara pressed herself back against her seat, holding her hands up to ward off the fiend.

But the creature simply hopped onto the sill and cocked its head, regarding her curiously. For many minutes, they stared at each other, then Chiara dared to move, straightening up. The familiar did not twitch.

'The queen's magic doesn't control you anymore, does it?' she asked softly so as not to wake her father.

The familiar chirruped, then attempted to keep its balance on the narrow ledge while it scratched behind its ear. This task achieved, it hopped into the box and clambered onto Chiara's lap. Even though the creature took great care, she could feel the tips of its talons even through her dress.

Once curled up on her lap, the familiar closed its eyes and started to give off a rattling wheeze that almost sounded like a cat's purr. Hesitantly, Chiara stroked the creature, and the wheeze got a little louder, perhaps even a little more contented.

'I think,' she said softly, 'I shall call you Franco. We shall be great friends, shall we not?' The creature looked up at her, eyes bleary with slumber, and a small smile crept over Chiara's lips.

The Watcher in the Woods

Fergus made a cup of coffee and sat down at the kitchen table. He blew on the drink, wanting to sip some moisture into his dry mouth. But the heat emanating from the cup promised a scalding if he tried.

Instead, he picked up the pen and stared at the notebook before him. It was of good quality with a smooth brown leather binding. Yet even though the paper was thick, he could still see lines on the current page where he'd crossed out yesterday's work on the previous one. The temptation to tear out that first, incoherent page was almost overwhelming.

What will future generations think of me if I can't even write a bloody introduction to what I do every day? But the words just hadn't come. How do you summarise a job that has been passed down from parent to child for almost two thousand years? One steeped in strangeness and death?

He looked out at the forest beyond his window, trying to find inspiration in the autumn colours, but his mind remained a blank.

With a sigh, he looked back at the book. *Well, maybe I should leave the introduction until last, or at least until later. Let's start with the history instead.*

He took a sip of his cooling coffee and began to write.

The Wood has been here for as long as anyone can remember. It belongs to no one and yet falls under the responsibility of four Watchers. We are stationed at four points around the Wood, roughly north, south, east, and west.

Being a Watcher runs in the family. I am writing this because I have no family left to pass the duty onto. I hope whoever reads this will

He stopped writing. Maybe that bit should go in the introduction. He sighed again, wishing this could be easier, wishing he'd had a family of his own so he could tell the history in person, like his father had done with him. Instead, he was forced to write it down to pass on to a stranger, or perhaps for some unknown person to find if he died suddenly in the Wood, which was always a possibility.

Leaving enough space for a couple of lines to finish off what he'd abandoned, he tried a new approach.

Many times, the Wood has escaped being cut down. With the continual push to provide affordable housing for the country, there have been some close calls. Although I've not seen any assessors during my Watching, my uncle did, and he told the story to my father, who passed it onto me.

A man from a building company came out and was taking measurements. My uncle spoke to him, and he seemed absolutely certain that his company would have the winning bid for the project. He wasn't going to cut it all down, just some of it, and build luxury apartments. He reckoned people would pay a lot for this desolate Scottish view.

My uncle was forced to leave him to it. When he next looked out of the window, the surveyor had vanished. My uncle hoped he'd gone home.

Fergus took another swallow of coffee. A fresh line of thought occurred to him. Turning to another page, he wrote at the top <u>About Me</u>.

The position of Watcher passes down through family members. It should have passed from my uncle to one of his two sons, but they were all three killed in a car crash. My cousins were just teenagers.

So my father had to take up the position. He visited the other three Watchers, dragging me with him, and they told him what they could. He took in far more than I did, but when I came of age, he told me all of what he'd learned during his decade of Watching.

My mother left us shortly after we moved into this lodge. She said she couldn't stand to be near the forest. I used to wake up at night and hear her weeping downstairs. For about six months after she left, I really hated her. But then I began to see more of the Lost Ones, and I realised that she hadn't meant to be cruel. She'd simply done the only thing she could to keep herself sane. If she'd stayed, I'm certain she'd have become a Lost One too, and I couldn't bear to find her during one of my tours of the forest. I still have nightmares about it, even at forty-one years old.

Fergus read back what he'd written and felt a tightness in his guts; this was all too personal. Fighting back frustration at not being able to finish anything, he flipped back to the previous page and began again.

As the afternoon wore on, my uncle did his usual tour of the perimeter of the forest. He found a car and saw letters inside addressed to the building company the man had mentioned. My uncle hurried back and gathered his tools before heading into the wood.

The surveyor was lucky as my uncle found him before the sun went down. But when they finally emerged from the Wood, it was dark, and my uncle said the man had seen things on their walk back that had made his face as white as the moon.

My uncle took him into the lodge where my aunt made the man some hot, sweet tea and forced him to eat a slice of ginger cake. They offered him a bed for the night, but the surveyor shot to his feet and said he wasn't staying a single minute longer near the Wood. Even though my uncle was concerned that the man was too shaken up to drive, he nevertheless took him back to his car. The surveyor drove away, weaving slightly from side to side.

No luxury apartments were ever built, and no one else has come knocking to ask about such things. I'm sure they will in time, but it seems a Watcher need do little to dissuade them. The Wood does that well enough, once they step into the gloom of it.

He put the pen down and flexed his fingers. He'd been gripping it too tightly. It felt wrong writing down these words with a modern plastic writing implement. Some deep part of him insisted it should be done with quill and ink. He'd tried that, however, and not only had it taken him twice as long to write a single sentence but the end result had been splotchy and unreadable. A plastic pen was the best he could do. While he acknowledged that it would be best of all to write it on a computer, he knew the words wouldn't sit right on an electronic screen.

By now, the sky outside was lighter. It was time to do his morning rounds before work.

The sun still gave out a decent bit of warmth, but the shadows held the cool promise of winter creeping closer. The trees were a riot of golds and browns, with some startling reds thrown in. Fergus tried to enjoy their rich colours and ignore the deep green of the pine trees. The Wood itself made him uneasy, but it was the pine trees that made him truly uncomfortable. He theorised that it was because they still seemed so alive in the dead of winter, a time when the Wood received its highest number of guests.

Fergus had found himself thinking of the Lost Ones as "guests" before they met their end. At that point, their condition was temporary, something he could rectify, if he was quick enough. The Wood's guests could be saved; Lost Ones could not.

Every tour Fergus undertook started the same way, with a tight knot in his belly that gradually eased if the tour brought up no abandoned vehicles or footsteps leading into the trees. If he did find such things, the knot tightened and his blood became icy cold.

Halfway round, Fergus stopped and took off the backpack he'd been carrying. He did some stretches, rotating his shoulder joint. It was aching after yesterday, when he and a wrench had been on the losing side of a fight with a tractor engine.

As his muscles relaxed, he looked out over the wide-open space before him. The nearest town was only twenty miles away, the nearest village a lot closer. But this section of the wood looked out over a wild rolling space where nothing lived. Ahead of him were hills and beyond that, civilisation again. But in this little pocket, he could imagine that he was the only one alive around here. Comforting, when you spent your mornings and evenings looking for the newly dead.

'That view is the only thing that makes this job worthwhile,' he muttered. Behind him, a tree branch creaked. Fergus turned, slowly, half-expecting to see a body swinging from a branch. But there was nothing there, and he let out a shaky breath.

'Time to move on, I think,' he said to himself, hoisting the backpack onto his shoulders again.

His round ended at the boundary line which divided his Watching Section from Alison's, the next one along. Tonight, he'd walk the other way to the other boundary, the one he shared with Peter.

He didn't know Peter very well – a sour man who kept to himself – but he'd shared a couple of cups of coffee with Alison. He'd once even thought that there might be something between them, and he'd been working himself up to ask her on a date when she'd introduced him to her new girlfriend, and he'd backed right off.

However, she'd taken to a strange little custom recently. The line between their boundaries was marked by the trunk of an old tree that had been gutted by lightning. There was a hollow nook in it, and on Christmas Day last year, the light had reflected off something metallic inside. Gingerly, he'd reached in and pulled out a little origami crane. It had been crafted from Christmas wrapping paper.

Standing there, in the freezing cold, holding a small piece of beautiful artwork in his hand, Fergus had chuckled. Then he'd laughed, then he'd bellowed and bent double. The laughter was an expulsion of all the stress and tension he'd felt over the lonely Christmas break. Other people had been with their family, sharing presents, eating turkey. He'd had a dozen cards and a couple of presents from work colleagues, and he'd eaten a pizza as the sun went down. It had been depressing and unbearably lonely. Then he'd had to face the Wood.

But the crane had been proof that someone had been thinking of him – most importantly, someone who understood his duties and the toll they took.

He'd gone straight home and looked up origami on the internet. He'd made a flower, a rather messy one, but he hoped the sentiment would be appreciated. The next day, he'd put it in the nook.

Since that bleak Christmas Day, Alison had left him a total of fifty-three little origami creatures. He'd cleared a shelf in the lodge for them, and whenever he felt lonely, he'd gone to look at them. In return, he'd given her about thirty, mainly because his work was so shoddy he almost felt embarrassed leaving them for her.

He'd met Alison a couple of times in the last year, mainly in the supermarket. Each time, he'd debated telling her just how much this simple exchange meant to him, but somehow it had seemed wrong to talk of the joy she'd brought him at such a bleak time while they were surrounded by canned soup and packet sauces.

There was no origami today, however, but since she'd left him a beautiful cat made of red wrapping paper only three days ago, he shouldn't be too disappointed.

He walked home faster than he'd come. When he got back, he checked the antique barometer on the wall and then checked it against the electronic one on the table nearby. They both offered up the same reading, and the knot in his stomach finally unwound. If they'd been different, he would have been obliged to walk to the other boundary marker between him and Peter before work, but if they were the same, that duty could wait until this evening.

Fergus was in on time and in a good mood. The local cafe was doing pumpkin coffee, something which Fergus had never thought he'd develop a taste for but which he found himself looking forward to each year as the seasons turned. He arrived in town with enough time to grab one before getting to work for nine. Sure, he was the boss, and his assistant mechanic didn't get in until nine-thirty, but there were standards to maintain even when no one was watching.

When he got back home that evening, he decided to do his tour to the other boundary marker before tea; then he could close the door on the day and relax with a beer in front of the football. The barometers still aligned with each other, and his walk was almost pleasant. In his years of Watching, he'd learned to detect a certain tension in the air when a guest had arrived. He wondered if he'd learned to recognise whatever affected the mechanical barometer. But tonight, all tension was missing, and he came back to the lodge relaxed.

He reheated some shepherd's pie and ate it in front of the TV. When half-time came, he went to make himself a cup of coffee. He felt restless and fidgety, unable just to stand there while his ancient kettle took an age to boil. He picked up the pen just as something to fiddle with, then found himself sitting down and opening the notebook again.

His intention had been merely to read through it, but a sentence had come into his head as he read the History section, and he felt he should put it down on paper before it vanished. One sentence turned into many.

When I first found out that I was to be a Watcher, I tried to find out everything I could about the Wood. I searched local bookshops, the library (even the British Library), newspaper cuttings, and the internet. You can find numerous lists of suicide spots all over the world if you know where to look, but two things struck me.

1. Most of the other suicide places were bridges or cliffs, where people would jump to their deaths, which kind of makes sense.

2. There was only one other forest I could find, in Japan, where people go to

commit suicide. But there was no mention of the Wood at all.

But the weirdest thing about the Wood is that I don't think all the Lost Ones in there actually committed suicide among the trees. Every Watcher finds bodies, and we have a good thing going with the local police. Seriously, I don't know why the Watchers haven't been arrested more often. I have two theories on that: either the Watchers are at the bottom of the command chain and there are people in the government who just slide the paperwork into a plain Manila envelope and tell the authorities to let us be (which makes me wonder if there are more places around the world like this that nobody knows about), or the Wood somehow looks after itself.

Anyway, the number of bodies I find is nowhere near the number of Lost Ones I see. I don't know where all these extra ghosts come from. Are they drawn to the Wood after death? If so, why? Have they visited it before? When I was a teenager, I had nightmares that just visiting the

Wood would draw you back here after death and that I was doomed to wander among the trees forever because I've been in it so often. I felt better after my dad pointed out that there are no ghosts of other Watchers in there.

But it still doesn't explain where the extra ghosts come from.

Another thing I couldn't figure out was: if you can't find a reference to the Wood anywhere online and only in a few local newspapers, how do people know to come here to commit suicide?

I've met people from Glasgow, Newcastle, London – even France and Portugal. How did they know to get here? I asked some of those who survived, but hardly anyone wants to talk about it. One man did though, and I've written down as much as I can remember.

"I was searching online for a holiday destination, somewhere not too far away. I just wanted a break from my job, which was shit at the time, and my ex-wife, who was shittier. The Wood came up as a pop-up advert, a local haven for peace and quiet. So, I booked a nearby hotel and thought I'd come visit, maybe do some sketching. But by the time I got here, my whole life had gone to hell in other even shittier ways.

"When I stood in front of the forest, it just felt right – more right than anything else in my life just then. I wanted to walk in and keep walking. I was sure when I came out the other side everything would be better. So, I went in, and I started walking and then... I saw things. Horrible things..."

I never found out what he saw, because he started to cry then. He howled and wept, and I genuinely thought he might choke or something. Then suddenly he just stopped. He stood up and said he had to get back to his hotel.

So, I don't know how people get here – either when they are alive or dead. All I know is the Watcher's Duty: to find the live ones and bring them out before it's too late, and to deal with the bodies of those you can't find in time. If you're reading this, then it's your duty now.

Fergus put the pen down and stared at the last line: *If you're reading this, then it's your duty now.* Who would read this? Just who was he writing it for? He lived with the daily fear that he would die somehow without passing on his knowledge. Would the other Watchers cover for him? Would they walk his routes until they found a replacement?

Would the Wood let them? What would happen if a section had no Watcher? Would the Lost Ones leave? Would more guests be drawn to the Wood, entering through the weak spot left by his death?

A shiver ran down his spine and he stood up abruptly. He'd wasted enough time on this. He might not die for years yet, and there was a football match going on that he should be enjoying.

The water in the kettle was only lukewarm now, so he abandoned the idea of coffee and went back to the TV. He wasn't supporting either team, but it was a good game nonetheless.

When the match was over, he started towards bed, but glancing into the kitchen had another idea popping into his head.

Fergus turned to a clean page and began to

write, wanting to capture the words before sleep stole them out of his head.

Granny Dumping

Yes, this is actually a thing. It's even in the dictionary. It's where someone dumps an elderly relative in a public place, especially a hospital, leaving no clue as to their identity. The elderly person is then taken in by the state and looked after. People do this to avoid having to pay healthcare costs that they can't afford.

That's the modern version, anyway. In the past, "granny dumping" was a lot more final.

There are lots of stories and fairy tales about babies being abandoned in forests or on hillsides by parents who can't afford to feed them, and then the babies are found and cared for by generous people and the child grows up to be a hero or something.

That's in fairy tales. In real life, babies were abandoned and left to starve or be killed by wild animals if their family couldn't afford to feed them. Same with old people — left out to wander around and die in places like the Wood.

My uncle felt sure that the Wood started out as a place where people were left to die.

Oh no, little baby.

Fergus's head jerked up. He'd heard a whisper, he was sure of it. He looked around the room, but it was empty. An old fear gripped him that one of the Lost Ones had wandered out of the Wood and was in his house. He'd once seen a Lost One at the edge of the Wood, a man who had died in there during the night, but the ghost had looked around in confusion and then wandered back into the trees.

Telling himself he was being ridiculous, he turned to a new page.

The Watcher's Pack

Every Watcher, when he goes into the Wood, must carry a pack containing several essential items. These include a hatchet small enough to cut down small trees and a coppicing knife to help with branches that get in your way. Sometimes guests get themselves wedged in somewhere and you need to cut them out.

A flashlight is essential if you go in at night, and a fresh bottle of water too. The paths in the Wood don't always lead where you think they do, and even Watchers can get lost.

There's also an ointment in a little tin. This is made from the bark of the trees and a red lichen that grows on it mixed with beeswax (there's a recipe on another page). If you rub this on anyone's eyes, it will give them the Sight (ie the ability to see ghosts). Generally, those who go into the Wood see the ghosts anyway. There are some who can't see them, and in most cases, that's a blessing. But as one Watcher found out, that can put a guest in even greater danger (see Malcolm and Ernest in The Record Book, 1806). Since then, all Watchers carry a small pot in case of

Please don't go in there.

Fergus jumped to his feet, knocking the chair over. 'Who's there?' Only silence answered him.

Hesitantly, he went to the window and pulled back the curtain. A childish fear rose up that he'd see the faces of the dead pressed against the glass, their eyes hungry for the warmth and his soul. But all that showed through the glass was the moonlit night outside.

He scanned the edge of the Wood, and his heart lurched when he saw movement. A figure was standing, looking up at the trees. He opened the door and called out, 'Hello? Can I help you?'

The figure turned his way and he felt a surge of relief; the dead normally ignored the living, unless they came into direct contact with them. As the figure hurried towards him, he could see that it was a woman in a thick coat buttoned up against the cold. Only when she stood before his back door, the light from inside illuminating her properly, did he recognise her. How could he ever forget the face of the woman who broke his heart?

'Nikki! What the hell are you doing here?'

Her face was white. 'My son. I think he went into the Wood.'

She has a son? Has it been so long? Did she forget me so completely?

He forced himself to concentrate on what was important, on what she'd said. 'Your son has gone into the Wood? Why? It wasn't a bet, was it?' Some of the local kids dared each other now and again to go into the Wood, and if they weren't too petrified when he'd extracted them, Fergus had been known to shout at them and call their parents, who shouted at them in turn.

Nikki looked down, her shoulder-length brown hair falling over her face. 'Kurt and I had an argument,' she said softly, 'a horrible, horrible argument, and Jonathan ran away.' She looked up, tears on her eyelashes. 'He's been bullied at school too. It's not like when we were young. There are so many different ways for kids to be shitty to each other now.' There was bitterness in her voice. 'Cyberbullying they call it. Ever heard of it?' He shook his head. 'They have messaging apps on their phones and can text you something horrible at three in the morning. Or they can take stupid videos, or send you screenshots of everyone slagging you off.

'I've been trying to help Jonathan through it, but Kurt took a "more robust view,"' there was scorn in her voice at that. 'He said they were picking on Jonathan because he was weak and he needed to man up. Kurt kept saying this over and over and he started screaming at the boy, calling him a pussy, and in the end I told him to stop, and he turned on me.' She clutched the coat tighter around herself. 'He was horrible, just... awful. I didn't know anyone could act like that. Then, when it was over, I turned round and Jonathan was gone.'

'So why did you think he'd come here?'

'I don't know. I just did. Something inside of me. Does that sound crazy?'

'Not really, unfortunately.'

'Maybe it's just because I was so scared he'd come here and end it all. You know, like the stories say about this place. But maybe he's not here. Maybe he's just run to a mate's house or something.'

Fergus reached out and squeezed the arm of her coat reassuringly. 'Maybe, but if so, he'll be safe there, won't he? So I can spend time looking around the Wood, just in case, yes?'

She nodded. 'So long as you meant to say "we" can spend time looking.'

'That's really not a good idea, Nikki. There are

things in the Wood, terrible, awful things that you could see...'

His words trailed off as she stepped closer to him. There was a sour stench about her, sweat and something else unpleasant that he couldn't quite identify. 'Do you think that telling me there are terrible, awful things where my son might be is going to make me less inclined to come, or more?'

He struggled not to take a step away from her stench and her determination. 'Point taken,' he said awkwardly. 'Let me grab my bag and a coat first.'

When he'd got what he needed, he left the house and locked up. Striding towards the Wood, Nikki fell into step behind him. As always, Fergus paused at the Wood's edge. Walking into it had to be a conscious, determined decision. You couldn't go rushing in.

'Why have we stopped?' Nikki asked.

'Just preparing. For a moment.' He turned to her. 'You ready?'

The fact that she glanced into the trees and hesitated reassured him that she was taking the threat of the Wood seriously. It increased his chances of getting her out again alive.

She nodded. 'Ready.'

As always, a little shudder ran down Fergus's neck as he stepped into the shadow of the trees. Even if the air was baking hot outside, among the trees it would be cold. There were no sunbeams in the Wood, nowhere that the sun's rays would penetrate fully. Instead, the Wood had a constant low level of light, a permanent gloom with no direct light source

But now they were venturing into the Wood at night, and the dark would be absolute. Fergus dug two torches out of his backpack and handed one to Nikki. 'Here. This'll help.'

She shook her head. 'I don't need it. I can see perfectly well. Can't you?'

He frowned at her and was about to disagree when he realised she was right. It was gloomy in here, but no less so than it was during the day.

Maybe the moon's particularly bright and directly overhead or something. It was an explanation, but not a particularly rational one. And the deepest part of his mind came up with another one: the Wood wants us to see something tonight.

His instincts told him to turn and run, but he couldn't bring himself to move. If Nikki's son was in here, Fergus had to find him.

'Jonathan!' Nikki's shout bounced around them, and Fergus winced.

'Don't shout, please.'

'Why not? How will he find us? Jonathan!'

'Trust me on this. Shouting is a bad idea. It'll bring the Lost Ones.' She stared at him, confused. 'Remember those stories we whispered when we were kids, about the Wood being haunted? Well, it is.'

He expected her to argue, but she just hung her head. 'Alright. I'm sorry.' When she raised her head again, there were tears glistening on her eyelashes. He had a sudden, overwhelming urge to reach out and wipe them away.

But she's not my girlfriend anymore. She chose Kurt over me. He gets to wipe away the tears, even if he bloody well caused them in the first place.

'Come on,' he said. 'Let's get going.'

Nikki didn't shout, but she kept repeating her son's name in a loud whisper as they walked. He tried to blank out her voice, concentrating on listening for any unusual sounds. Then he realised she'd been talking to him.

'What?'

'I said, what exactly is it you do here?'

He hesitated. 'What do *you* think I do?'

'My grandmother always told me that your grandfather then your uncle was the person to go to if ever anyone was lost. I remember, back when I was a little girl, one of the teachers from a nearby school went missing. One of my friends had gone to that school before she joined ours, so I vaguely recognised the name. A few days later, my friend was in tears, saying her old teacher had died, in the Wood. I tried to ask my parents about it, but they wouldn't tell me. She was called Shirley Hill, I think. Do you remember at all?'

An image came into Fergus's mind of a woman with white foam speckled pink running down her chin. Her eyes were sunken and full of loss.

'Yes. I remember. It was an overdose, I think.'

'Yeah, I found that out later, when I was older. But you haven't answered my question. What's the connection between your family and this place?'

'I... watch the Wood. For people going in. I try to stop them. And if I can't, I bring out their corp—' He clamped his mouth shut.

Silence lay between them for a while, the only sound the crunch of their footsteps and Nikki's sniffs as she tried to stifle tears. Then she cleared her throat and said, 'But you work as a mechanic as well, don't you? My father says you're one of the best around.'

'Yeah, well, it pays the bills.'

'It pays the bills, while your true job is this, you mean?'

He gave a snort of laughter. 'I guess. When did you get so insightful?'

She laughed. It was a wonderful sound, a moment of joy piercing the gloom. 'I took an online psychology course. You know, one of those internet deals. I learned a lot.' Her face fell. 'For example, I learned to recognise that Kurt was a manipulating bastard.'

That final statement hung heavily between them. Fergus was trying to think of what to say when Nikki gave out a choked cry. He spun round and followed her line of sight.

Standing a little way off the path, with his back to them, was a boy. He was dressed in a plum-coloured blazer and grey trousers. He looked like any normal boy, except half his head was missing where he'd blown it off with a shotgun. The gun was rusted and long gone, only his mangled soul remained.

'Oh god, oh god,' Nikki gasped.

Fergus pulled her away. The coat sleeve felt cold in his grip, and he realised she must be freezing.

'Keep walking. Don't look back. Come on, Nikki, you can do this.'

'Oh god. Who was he?'

'His name was Michael. There was a private school a couple of miles away in the eighteen-hundreds. Do you remember we did a history project on it?' She didn't answer but he continued anyway. 'Michael went there and when his mother died, he got the groundsman's shotgun and shot himself.'

'Oh.'

Fergus knew what she was thinking: is my son here, like that? Is that what he'll look like when we find him?

'Can we go any faster?' she asked.

'Sure.'

It was a further five minutes before they encountered another Lost One. The ghosts didn't often move from their places, so it should – theoretically – be possible to avoid them. But Fergus had often followed the forest path round a bend and come across a Lost One he'd deliberately planned a route to avoid. When he took his bearings, he would realise he wasn't where he thought he was. He suspected that the Wood shifted the path. It was a crazy idea when considered in bright daylight, but among the towering trees it seemed only too plausible.

This time, Fergus knew it was coming because he always recognised what he called Bolton's Tree. He turned to Nikki and said, 'The path is going to curve round in a minute. I want you to keep your eyes straight ahead. Do *not* look at the tree.'

'Okay.'

'I mean it.'

'Alright,' she said, irritated.

He nodded and gestured that she should go first.

To Fergus's mind, what made the Lost Ones both so terrifying and heart-wrenchingly pitiful was how real they looked. As a child, he'd borrowed a book from the library called *Mysteries of the Unknown*. There had been several photographs of ghosts in there, but they'd been pathetic, colourless things. Some were no more than black or white smudges.

But the Lost Ones in the Wood looked solid

enough to touch. They weren't, of course. That was how Fergus told the difference between Lost Ones and mere guests. A guest was still flesh and blood; you could take their arm and lead them away. But your hand would pass straight through a Lost One – when you first touched them, anyway.

Fergus kept his gaze lowered while still keeping an eye on Nikki ahead. She was walking with her head down, but the creak of the rope startled her.

Don't look, don't look, Fergus willed her, but she looked. They always did.

'Oh god,' she said, her voice thick.

Fergus knew what she was seeing without needing to look himself: a man with a noose around his neck, swaying gently in a breeze that only he felt. His face was pale and swollen, making his black lips and the even blacker tongue protruding from them seem so much more unnatural.

The ghost's clothes were tatty, his jeans stained where his bowels had voided in his final moments. His body was perfectly motionless; not even his fingers twitching. But his eyes constantly roved about, as if his soul was stuck in there, searching for a way out.

Fergus had suffered many nightmares about Sam Bolton and his tree when he was a teenager. He'd dreamt that Sam had used sharp nails to cut himself down, his legs crumpling as he hit the ground. Then he had crawled all the way to the lodge, up the stairs, and into Fergus's bedroom. His restless eyes were still scanning all round as he shuffled towards the bed. Fergus always woke up, often screaming, at the point where Sam's gaze stilled, locked on Fergus, and a terrible grin twisted the cadaver's black lips.

Fergus gently pushed Nikki on. She moved, but reluctantly; her steps now seemed uneven, as if she was drunk, or in shock.

'Who was that?' she asked eventually.

'Sam Bolton. He was a jilted lover, I think, although the Record Book isn't clear.'

'The Record Book?' Her face was slack, but he could see a little life in her eyes still, as if her essence was trying to claw its way back to the surface through the black void it had sunk into.

'There's a book; we call it the Record Book. When someone goes into the Wood and doesn't come out, the Watcher records their name. He finds out as much about them as he can – how they lived, how they died. Then it's noted for all time, and future Watchers can know what they're facing. It helps Watchers tell the difference between Lost Ones and g— I mean, real people without having to touch them.'

'Touch them?'

'Your hand will pass straight through a Lost One, while a living person is solid. But you don't want to touch Lost Ones if you can avoid it.'

'Why not?'

A memory rose in his mind, of when he'd seen Rosamund Mundy. It had been his third trip into the Wood. He knew Rosamund from school; she was a few years older than him, but he'd seen her in the playground.

He'd been walking with his father and then she was just there. His father went on ahead and Fergus was going to call out, but the sight of Rosamund had him fixed to the spot. She'd been staring down at her slender pale arms which ended in bloody wrists. The blood was pouring out of her onto the ground. He'd rushed forward, thinking he could save her if he gripped both her wrists. But his hands passed straight through her.

Her head snapped up, her wide eyes locking on him. 'Help me,' she said. 'I didn't mean to do it. I just wanted to stop it hurting so much. Please, you have to help me, please...' She'd staggered towards him then, and although he'd backed away, he hadn't been fast enough. She crashed into him and they went tumbling to the ground. Her weight had pressed down on him, and he'd felt the cold wetness of her blood soaking through his clothes. It was only a moment later that his father had pulled him free, but to Fergus, trapped beneath a corpse and looking into its pleading eyes, the experience had felt like it lasted a lifetime.

'If you touch them, they come after you. And they become solid. I don't think they want to hurt you. I think they want you to save them. But that's bad enough.'

'Because you can't save them?

'Because you can't save them.'

They kept on in silence for another half an hour, and then something on the wind caught Fergus's attention. He stopped and gestured for Nikki to do the same. Slowing his breathing, he listened carefully until he heard it again. Sobbing. It was the sweetest, most human sound he could wish to hear.

'This way!' He charged ahead along a tiny path that branched off from the main one.

'Hello?' came a small voice from up ahead.

Nikki streaked past him, calling out, 'Johnathan!'

The trees quickly thinned, and they came to a small clearing with a boulder in it. Curled up against the boulder was a young boy, no more than twelve years old.

Nikki slumped to her knees and held out her arms. 'Jonathan! Oh, my boy.'

Jonathan's eyes widened when he saw them and he scrambled to his feet. He raced forward, passing straight through his mother and wrapping his arms around Fergus's waist.

'I'm sorry, I'm so sorry, I didn't mean to come in here, but Kurt was so horrible, he hurt my mum and I didn't know what to do or where to go and so I came here because there are ghosts and I thought if she was really dead then I'd find her but she's not here so she can't be dead and now I can't find my way out and I'm so scared and... and...' His voice was swept away by his sobs.

Fergus stared at Nikki, horror creeping through him. She stood up, avoiding his eyes.

Very slowly, she undid the top buttons of her coat, revealing a dark wet stain on her chest.

The coat. I touched it. It was real. But she wasn't. She put on a coat, and I couldn't tell the difference. How did she even know to do that? How can the dead wear clothes?

Nikki looked up at him. 'Thank you for finding him. I couldn't bear to think that he would be trapped in here.'

'But you... you're—'

'Yes, I know.' Her tone was resigned while her eyes were filled with utter desolation.

'Where did you get the coat?'

'It's mine. I don't know. I was in the kitchen and then I was here, well, I was outside, where you found me.'

Jonathan pulled away and looked up at him. 'Who are you talking to?'

'I... a ghost.'

He swallowed then whispered, 'Is it my mum?'

He thought about lying, then said, 'Yes.'

'Where? I can't see her.'

'No, it takes a special gift to see the dead, or...'

'Or what?' The boy's face was so full of hope that it made Fergus's heart ache.

'An ointment. All Watchers carry it. We make it from the Wood itself. You put it on your eyes and you can see the dead.' It felt foolish saying out loud, although it had sounded perfectly rational when his father had sat him down and explained it.

'I want some,' Jonathan said quietly.

Fergus knelt down, looked the boy in the eyes. 'I know you miss her, but you don't want to see your mother. Not like this. It'll haunt you.'

Tears were shining in Jonathan's eyes. 'Please,' he whispered. 'I didn't get to say goodbye. I don't care what she looks like. I won't even turn around. Please. I just want to say goodbye.'

'Please.' Nikki's whisper was little more than a gentle breeze. 'If there's anything you can do, please do it.'

An agony of indecision raged through Fergus. He had it in his power to grant this wish, but it wasn't just a momentary thing. If he gave the boy the ability to see his mother, he'd see ghosts forever. It was a kind gift with a cruel legacy.

But all his hesitation was swamped by the look of pleading in Nikki's eyes. He had never been able to say no to her before and he couldn't start now. 'Fine,' he said reluctantly. He opened his backpack and got out the small tub. 'I want you to close your eyes, Jonathan, and not open them until I say so. Do you promise?'

'I promise.

'Do you *swear*?'

'I swear.'

'Good.' He applied a thin layer of the waxy substance to Jonathan's eyes then got up and went over to Nikki. His hands were shaking as he reached out and he paused, just for a moment, before buttoning up her coat. He marvelled at how solid it was. 'Better if he doesn't see,' he said softly. She nodded and he said to Jonathan, 'You can open your eyes now.'

The boy did so and instantly ran to his mother. Fergus walked a little way away. This was not something that he should be a part of.

He sat on a tree trunk, fiddling with the pot in his hands, trying not to listen to the whispers and stifled sobs behind him. In the undergrowth, a little way off, was a half-buried skull. He wondered which of the Lost Ones it belonged to.

Nikki called his name and he went back.

Jonathan still had his arms around her, his face buried in the coat. Nikki looked at Fergus with eyes bright and shimmering with tears.

I didn't know the dead could cry.

'I've something to tell you,' she said solemnly. 'Jonathan is Kurt's child. But...' she hesitated, looking incredibly uncomfortable, 'I put you down as the father on his birth certificate.'

'What the hell? Why?'

'You're the father he should have had. I can't say what made me put your name down, a moment of whimsy maybe.'

Above him, a breeze made the leaves rustle. Fergus thought of the Wood, of how it always seemed to have four Watchers. He thought of how his father, when he was drunk once, had talked about suspecting the Wood had caused the death of his brother because he was slacking in his duties. Now Fergus wondered whether the Wood had known he wouldn't have a family and had lined up a replacement. The thought made him sick.

'I don't know why I did it, but I'm glad I did.' Her voice hardened and a gleam came into her eyes. 'He can't go back to Kurt, he can't. Do you understand?'

'But you must have other family.'

'My mother died, and my father cut off all contact years ago. There is no one else.' Her voice dropped to a whisper. 'Just you. Please, Fergus, I know I have no right to ask this of you, but please, look after my boy.'

Fergus hesitated. Jonathan could move away, live with Nikki's father maybe. There was no reason for him to be bound to this life. He could go to a decent school, university even. He could be anything he wanted.

If he stayed with Fergus, he'd be doomed to serve the Wood.

He might still have said no, even though he could never deny Nikki anything, but then Jonathan twisted his head slightly, looking at Fergus through one puffy red eye. When he spoke, his voice was quiet but firm. 'Please let me stay with you. Just for a bit. I don't want to go back to Kurt, not after...' He stopped, breathing hard, but not crying.

Fergus looked at Jonathan, who had entered the Wood as a twelve-year-old kid and now seemed suddenly so much older. He sighed. 'Okay. Come back with me. You can stay the night, at least. We'll see what the police say and social services, and I guess, if they can't find you anywhere else...'

In the silence, a tear ran down Nikki's cheek, landing on Jonathan's hair. 'Thank you,' she whispered, and then she was gone. There was no puff of smoke or blinding light, she was just there one moment, and the next Jonathan was holding an empty coat.

He thought the boy might start screaming – he knew he would have done. But instead, Johnathan wiped his eyes and walked over to Fergus. Clutching the coat tightly, he said, 'Now what?'

~

It had been a long, tiring walk back through the Wood, and then Fergus had to face the task of calling the police. He asked to speak to the chief inspector, Robert Stuart, a man he'd dealt with before and, most importantly, a local who knew all about the Wood. Fergus gave him all the details, knowing that Robert would use his discretion as to what he passed on to his officers and what made it into the final report.

'I'll come myself,' Robert said then hung up.

Fergus had made Jonathan a cup of hot

chocolate before he went to the phone; when he returned to the kitchen, the drink was untouched and a layer of skin had formed on the top of it.

He sat down with a sigh and said, 'Well, that's done. The chief inspector will be here shortly and we can ask him what to do then.'

Jonathan looked up, his eyes wide. 'But they won't take me back to Kurt, will they?'

'Send a young boy to a suspected murderer? Probably not, no. But they might send you to your grandfather's, I suppose. Or a friend's house. After all, I barely know you.'

'Mum told me I'd be safe with you,' Jonathan said, that steel back in his voice again. 'She said she put your name down on my birth certificate, that you were the father I should have had. I want to stay here.'

He looked down at his cup, clenching and unclenching his fists. Then he said quietly, 'Mum always said I reminded her of someone she once knew. She said I reminded her of the best man in her life. Of course, she never said those things in front of Kurt. He wouldn't have liked it. But she told me, in the Wood, that I reminded her of you.'

He looked up and met Fergus's eyes. Silence

stretched between them, and Fergus could almost feel the future closing in around him, as if it was some tangible thing that had cocooned him so he was unable to escape. In that moment, he knew the boy was here to stay.

Jonathan broke eye contact and looked at the table. He pointed at the notebook. 'What are you writing?'

'A book. About the job I do.'

'Oh? About cars? Mum said you were a mechanic. I like cars.'

'Do you?'

Jonathan gave a small smile. 'Yeah. When I was a kid, I pulled my scooter apart and put it back together again. Didn't work as well, but it kind of started something, you know?'

'Yeah, I did something similar. Only it was with my father's motorbike. I didn't put it back together so well.'

'Was he mad at you?'

'To begin with. But he was a tinkerer himself, and he actually came to enjoy spending Sunday afternoons showing me how mechanical stuff worked. It was our time together.'

Jonathan's face fell. 'You're lucky. I wish I'd had someone to do that with me. Kurt would never have...' He stared at his mug again, mute and miserable.

An unspoken offer lay on Fergus's tongue like a bitter seed.

If I say it, then the matter is sorted. There'll be no going back. He glanced out of the window at the Wood that had stood for thousands of years, that had protected itself in more ways than he knew.

Fergus looked back at Jonathan and the words came before he could stop them. 'Well, perhaps you and I could make Sunday afternoons our thing. You know, if you choose to stay. And if they let you.'

Jonathan grinned; like Nikki's smile in the forest, it was a moment of joy that lit up the darkness. 'I'd like that.'

Jonathan reached out and picked up the hot chocolate. He pushed the skin aside then drank it down in five big gulps. Wordlessly, Fergus picked up the cup and took it over to the sink. He looked out of the window again at the Wood. The night was still, the dead flower stalks in his window boxes motionless. But the leaves on the trees shook in an unseen wind, and even through the glass, Fergus thought he could hear distant, triumphant laughter.

Author's
Note

Hessian Sky

The first story in this book is based on the Russian fairy tale 'The Soldier and Death'. Those of us who grew up watching *Jim Henson's Storyteller* series will no doubt be familiar with it, but for those who aren't, here is a short recap.

A kindly soldier coming home from the war has only three biscuits left in his pack. Nevertheless, he gives those biscuits to three different beggars he meets on the road, and in return they give him the ability to whistle, a pack of lucky playing cards, and an enchanted sack. The last beggar tells the soldier that he has only to say "If this is a sack, then get in it" and whatever he is talking to will be trapped inside the sack.

During his journeys, the soldier comes across a castle which has been abandoned. No one can spend the night in there without falling prey to a group of devils who plague it every night with their singing and gambling.

The soldier spends the night there and meets the devils. He challenges them to cards and, using his lucky pack, he wins. The devils are furious and are about to attack him when he asks them, 'What is this?'

'A sack,' they reply.

'If this is a sack, then get in it,' the soldier cries, and all the devils are trapped.

After he's beaten them about quite a bit, the devils are begging for mercy. They agree to leave the castle and never return if only he will let them out.

The soldier goes on to have other adventures, and I just invented an extra one for him.

I always felt rather sorry for the soldier; he doesn't deserve the ending that he got in the original fairy tale, and certainly didn't deserve the ending that I gave him. But then, "happily ever after" isn't the only fairy tale ending around.

~

A Wolf in the House

Little Red Riding Hood is a tale that always scared me and Angela Carter's 'The Company of Wolves' was the first story that introduced me to the idea that fairy tales could be dark. In earlier versions of the story, before Perrault set it down as morality tale, the woodcutter was a much darker character and sometimes took Little Red Riding Hood to be his bride after saving her. That made me wonder if maybe the real monster wasn't necessarily the wolf, who was just trying to find himself a solid meal.

~

The Wild Hunt

This is the only reprint in this collection; the story first appeared on the Spinetinglers website and then in their anthology.

The Wild Hunt is a British legend and each region has its own special huntsman, from Sir Walter Raleigh to Odin or King Arthur. Also known as The Host, this collection of hunters ranges from the savage to the mischievous.

I set this story at Christmas, my favourite

time of year for ghost stories. I just love the juxtaposition of the cheery colours and twinkling fairy lights with the darkness which could hold so many horrors.

Rowan Cottage was also based on a real cottage I stayed in when I was child. I grew up in the countryside, so was used to wide open spaces, but this cottage had an unfenced back garden that just ended with a massive wood. Seeing the epitome of nature nestled up against the civilisation of a cottage garden without any boundaries between the two left a lasting impression on me, always reminding me that darkness and mystery are right on the edges of the civilisation we have created for ourselves.

~

Teeth in the Shadows

This story comes from a book of German legends which the Grimm brothers collected but chose not to use in their seminal work *Kinder und Hausmärchen*. In the legend, Emperor Charlemagne has a bell put up that anyone can ring if they require justice. It is rung by a serpent who leads Charlemagne to its nest where a toad is sitting on its eggs. Charlemagne considers the matter, declares that the toad is in the wrong, and has the toad burnt.

A few days later, the serpent presents Charlemagne with a special gem which Charlemagne gives to his wife. Turns out that this gem has the power to create longing in the donee for the person who possesses the gem, so Charlemagne is always longing for his wife when he's away.

Knowing the power of this gem, Charlemagne's wife doesn't want another to have it after her death because then Charlemagne will forget her. So, on her deathbed she hides it under her tongue. Although she dies and is buried, Charlemagne cannot be without her, so he has her body exhumed and the corpse travels with him wherever he goes.

An end is brought about when a young courtier hears about the powers of the gem and removes it from the wife's corpse. He puts it in his pocket at which point Charlemagne's affection turns towards the courtier.

Exasperated by the emperor's constant attention, the courtier throws the stone into a nearby set of hot springs. Although the great power of the gem is at an end, Charlemagne nevertheless felt a strong affiliation with the place where the stone had been cast, and he founded the city of Aachen there, which was to become his favourite residence.

~

The Watcher in the Woods

This is my own unique story, my own fairy tale, because it felt wrong to steal *all* my ideas for this book. If it has any grounding, then it's likely to lie in Aokigahara, a forest in Japan. However, many European fairy tales involve a wood or the wilderness in some form, and chart how normal humans deal with the creatures they find in there.

But strictly speaking, the Wood isn't based on anything, and it doesn't exist. Probably.

~

General thanks

Writing a book is a solitary occupation, but it does need a lot of extra-manuscript support, so to speak.

A huge thank you to Penny Jones, who beta-read this in record time and found some silly mistakes I'd missed over several readings.

Thanks are also due to Margrét Helgadóttir and Johann Thorsson who helped me out with the descriptions of Iceland. Anything that appears wrong or out of place is either down to my mistake or demonic forces at work in the story.

You wouldn't be reading this book if not for the patience and kindness of Steve Shaw who invited me to put down some words for him and then said they were good enough to publish.

Thanks to my mum, who always says kind things about my work.

And finally, thank you to my husband and daughter who lose me quite regularly to the office to dream up other people and their terrible deaths. I love you both.

Also by Charlotte Bond:

Novellas
Monstrous (Hersham Horror Press, 2017)
The Poisoned Crow (2019)

Now available and forthcoming from
Black Shuck Shadows:

Shadows 1 – The Spirits of Christmas
by Paul Kane

Shadows 2 – Tales of New Mexico
by Joseph D'Lacey

Shadows 3 – Unquiet Waters
by Thana Niveau

Shadows 4 – The Life Cycle
by Paul Kane

Shadows 5 – The Death of Boys
by Gary Fry

Shadows 6 – Broken on the Inside
by Phil Sloman

Shadows 7 – The Martledge Variations
by Simon Kurt Unsworth

Shadows 8 – Singing Back the Dark
by Simon Bestwick

Shadows 9 – Winter Freits
　　　　by Andrew David Barker

Shadows 10 – The Dead
　　　　　　by Paul Kane

Shadows 11 – The Forest of Dead Children
　　　　by Andrew Hook

Shadows 12 – At Home in the Shadows
　　　　by Gary McMahon

Shadows 13 – Suffer Little Children
　　　　　by Penny Jones

Shadows 14 – Shadowcats
　　　　　　by Anna Taborska

Shadows 15 – Flowers of War
　　　　by Mark Howard Jones

Shadows 16 – The Watcher in the Woods
　　　　by Charlotte Bond

Shadows 17 – Voices
　　　　　　by Kit Power

Shadows 18 – The Adventures of Mr Polkington
by Tina Rath

Shadows 19 – Green Fingers
by Dan Coxon

Shadows 20 – Three Mothers, One Father
by Sean Hogan

Shadows 21 – Uneasy Beginnings
by Simon Kurt Unsworth &
Benjamin Kurt Unsworth

blackshuckbooks.co.uk/shadows

Printed in Great Britain
by Amazon

67328522R00119